RUNNING THROUGH BEIJING

RUNNING THROUGH BEIJING

Xu Zechen
Translated by Eric Abrahamsen

Two Lines Press

跑步穿过中关村 © 2008 by Xu Zechen
Translation © 2014 by Eric Abrahamsen

Published by Two Lines Press
582 Market Street, Suite 700, San Francisco, CA 94104
www.twolinespress.com

ISBN 978-1-931883-36-8

Library of Congress Control Number: 2014934779

Design by Ragina Johnson
Cover Design by Andrew Walters

Printed in the United States of America

3 5 7 9 10 8 6 4

This project is supported in part by an award from
the National Endowment for the Arts.

ART WORKS.
arts.gov

1

I'm out.

As Dunhuang opened his mouth to shout, a dust devil rose up and filled his eyes, nose, and mouth with fine grit, obliging him to sneeze and rub his eyes. The little iron gate clanged shut behind him. He spat the sand from his mouth. The dust devil had already moved on. Tilting his head back he looked at the sky, a blur of yellow dust behind which the sun glowed, mild but rough, like a polished piece of ground glass or a copper mirror that had seen years of use. The sunlight had no power to dazzle, but it still made Dunhuang's eyes tear up—it was sunlight, after all. Another dust devil leaned toward him and he dodged out of its way. It was a sandstorm, he'd heard of them on the inside. They'd talked of only two things over the past few days: his getting out, and the sandstorms. In jail, he'd seen the storms picking up, seen the yellow dust settling on the steps and windowsills, but there wasn't enough room inside for it to really get going. If he could, he'd like to go back and tell that pack of old cabbage heads that if they wanted a real sandstorm, they had to get out into the wide open spaces.

Wild land stretched before him: a few trees showed new buds, but there was no green grass in sight. It must be buried by sand, Dunhuang thought, and kicked at the dry weeds beside the gate—he looked around but still couldn't see a speck of green. He'd been in jail three whole months, for Christ's sake, and not one green blade of grass had grown. It was cold with the wind on him, and he pulled a jacket out of his bag. Shouldering the bag, he shouted, "I'm out!"

The iron gate rasped and a head peered out. Dunhuang saluted it, then laughed and said, "What are you looking at? Back to your post."

The head glared at him, retracted, and the iron gate clanged shut once more.

Dunhuang walked for twenty minutes, then waved a little truck over. The driver, sporting a first growth of fluffy beard, asked where he was going. Dunhuang said anywhere was fine as long as it was in Beijing. The driver dumped him on west Fourth Ring Road; he was taking his truck to sell at the Liulangzhuang automobile market. As he got out, Dunhuang thought he recognized the place, that he'd been there before. He walked south, turned right, and, sure enough, there was a little corner store where he'd once bought some Zhongnanhai cigarettes. Sandstorm aside, Beijing hadn't changed much. Dunhuang felt a bit calmer; he had worried that the city might have transformed behind his back. He bought a pack of cigarettes and asked the young clerk if she recognized him. The girl smiled perfunctorily and said he looked familiar. He said, "I once bought four packs of cigarettes here."

As he was leaving, he heard the girl spit the melon-seed shells from her mouth and mutter, "Asshole."

Dunhuang didn't look back—*you're too ugly to argue with.* He followed the street, knowing he must look like a hoodlum; he started swinging his bag and swaggering down the wrong side of the street. He went slowly, savoring a Zhongnanhai. Being in jail was like being home in that it was hard to get a smoke. The first time he'd brought two cartons of Zhongnanhais home his father had been thrilled and passed them out to guests, solemnly telling them: Zhongnanhai, named after where the leaders of our nation live—they all smoke these.

Where the leaders of our nation live. Dunhuang had only passed the front gate of Zhongnanhai once before, on his way to see the flag-raising at Tiananmen. He'd dragged himself up at 4 am. Bao Ding had sworn at him and said, "You can see the flag raising any day, why do it on a foggy day?" It had been foggy, and that morning they had to make a delivery, but Dunhuang couldn't help himself. He hadn't been hustling with Bao Ding in Beijing long, and aside from enormous heaps of cash he dreamed of nothing but that flag, fluttering in the wind. He heard the clacking of the ceremonial guards' foot-steps as they passed in perfect unison through his dreams. As he flew toward Tiananmen that morning on a wrecked old bicycle, he passed a bright, blurry gate, where a few guards might have been standing, but he thought nothing of it. When he got back home, Bao Ding told him that was Zhongnanhai, and he regretted not having stopped. He always meant to go back and take a closer look, but never got around to it. It was like Bao Ding said, "You can go any day, so you end up going no day." He never went.

Dunhuang didn't know where he was headed. That seemed awful, when he thought about it. No place to go. The whole lot of them had gone to jail: Bao Ding, Big Mouth, Xin'an, Thirty Thou with the lame leg. Hardly anyone he knew was left; he'd have trouble just finding a place to crash. And he was short of money, he only had fifty on hand, minus the nine he'd just spent on cigarettes. For now, he'd follow his feet, and worry about the rest tomorrow—he could always just burrow in somewhere for the night. The sun was dropping steadily in the sandpaper sky, down toward the end of the street—looking more and more like a giant millstone weighing on Beijing's shoulders. Dunhuang took the cigarette from his mouth and whistled a bit to buck his spirits—this wouldn't kill him. When he was first in Beijing, that time he'd gotten separated from Bao Ding, hadn't he slept a night against a concrete pillar under an overpass?

Obstetrics Hospital. Zhongguancun Human Resources Center. The Bai Family Courtyard Restaurant. The Earthquake Bureau. He looked up and saw Haidian bridge in front of him. He hadn't meant to come this way. He stopped, watching a double-jointed bus run a red light under the bridge. He hadn't come here on purpose, but there wasn't anywhere he wanted to go. It was under Haidian Bridge that they'd been caught, he and Bao Ding. They had run all the way here from Pacific Digital City without stopping for breath, but still hadn't been able to shake the police. They'd still had their stuff with them. If they had known they were going to get nabbed they would have ditched it. He'd called to Bao Ding, "It's okay, these cops are too fat to buckle their pants." But the policemen turned out to be pretty nimble. A car had cut them off, and by then it was too late to toss anything.

That was three months ago. It had still been cold, around the New Year, the wind had sung in his ears. As they had sprinted and dodged they'd nearly made two cars collide under the bridge. Now he was out, but Bao Ding was still in jail. Bao Ding's left hand had been stomped on by the police. Dunhuang wondered if it was better.

Dunhuang turned onto another street, then turned again. The wind picked up more sand from the ground and he ducked in next to a building. The light was fading, it was almost dark. As he swatted the dust from his clothes, a girl carrying a bag like his walked up to him and said, "Want a DVD, mister?" She pulled a handful of movies from her bag. "I've got everything: Hollywood, Japanese, Korean, domestic hits. Also, classics and Oscar winners. Everything." She spread out the colorful movies for him to see. In the failing light, the colors were somehow lurid, but he knew that the movies were clean. Just like the girl. Dunhuang couldn't guess her age, maybe twenty-four or twenty-five? Maybe twenty-eight? No more than thirty. Thirty-year-old DVD-sellers didn't look like that; they carried children, they asked in furtive tones, "Hey, want a DVD? I've got all sorts; if you want porn I've got hi-def." Then they quickly drew the movies from their clothing.

"Even if I bought one I have nowhere to watch it," Dunhuang said to her, and leaned back against the wall to avoid another gust of passing sand.

"They'll play on a DVD player or a computer," the girl said. "They're cheap, I'll give you a deal, six kuai per movie."

Dunhuang dropped his bag on the steps, wanting to sit and rest. The girl thought he meant to buy and squatted down with him, pulling a sheet of newspaper from her bag and spreading out the DVDs. "They're all good, guaranteed high quality."

Dunhuang thought it would be impolite not to buy, and said, "All right, I'll take one."

"Thanks. Which one do you want?"

"Anything, as long as it's good."

The girl stopped and looked at him. "If you really don't want one then don't bother."

"Who said I don't want one?" He was laughing at himself now. "I'll take two! Hell, give me three!" He quickly rummaged through the movies under the building's lights.

The Bicycle Thief. Cinema Paradiso. Address Unknown.

"Hey, you're a film buff!" Excitement was obvious in her voice. "Those are classics!"

Dunhuang said he didn't really understand film, he'd picked them nearly at random. It was true, he didn't understand film. He had seen *The Bicycle Thief* before, and he'd once heard a pair of college students talking about *Cinema Paradiso* on the bus—the boy saying it was good, the girl saying it was great. He'd picked *Address Unknown* merely because the name seemed awkward; he wondered why it wasn't *Unknown Address*.

The DVDs bought, he sat on the steps looking at the neon lights on the building across the street. Four characters: "Hai Dian Chess Academy." He'd seen that name many times before. He drew out a cigarette, lit it, and blew a cloud of smoke toward the sign.

The girl packed the other DVDs into her bag and stood up, saying, "Aren't you going?"

"You go on, I'm going to rest a bit." Dunhuang saw no need to tell a stranger that he had no place to go.

She said goodbye and walked off, but then came back and sat on the step beside him. Dunhuang unconsciously shifted to make room.

"Got another?" She meant a cigarette.

Dunhuang looked at her, surprised. He passed her the pack and lighter. She made a comment about the mildness of Zhongnanhai. He had no cause to disagree. He'd crossed paths with many, many people during his time in Beijing, but his interactions with them were nearly all transactions, conducted for the sake of cash, and the girl's behavior threw him off balance. He only felt uneasy for a second, though—what could possibly go wrong? The barefoot don't fear the shod. Whatever happens, happens. Suddenly relaxed, he asked, "How's business?"

"Business is business. Weather's bad." The sandstorm had driven all the idlers indoors, and it was mostly idlers who bought DVDs.

"Mmm." Dunhuang nodded in sympathy. The weather affected his line of work, too. Rain or wind sent the world scurrying; no one was in the mood.

She was no stranger to cigarettes—her smoke rings were better than his. The two of them sat there, watching the sky darken. The pedestrians thinned out. Dunhuang heard someone in a nearby bookstore say, "Close it up, who's going to buy books when the gravel's flying?" Then there was the sound of a gate rattling down and banging into the ground. *Flying gravel... Hardly.* Dunhuang did his best not to look at the girl. All of a sudden he wasn't sure how to talk to her, he wasn't used to lounging around with girls he didn't know. What, exactly, was this turning into? He wanted to leave.

"What do you do?" the girl asked him abruptly.

"What do you think?"

"A student? I can't tell."

"I don't do anything. I'm homeless." Dunhuang found the truth was as easy as a lie.

"I don't believe you," she said, standing, "but even if you are homeless, let's have a couple of drinks. My treat."

Dunhuang smiled. *You've showed your hand now*, he thought. *I knew selling DVDs couldn't be your only profession.* He'd never even had sex, let alone paid for it, but Bao Ding and Three Thou had, and he had a basic grasp of the process. But a girl like this in that line of work...it was heartbreaking. Though the newspapers said many prostitutes were actually college students. Even college students—such a grand thing to be—had to sell themselves. Dunhuang once again pictured furtive women with their babies, selling movies.

"Why don't I treat you?" Dunhuang said, throwing caution to the wind. What the hell. "I don't know this area, you pick a spot."

2

They went to a hotpot restaurant called Ancients next to Changchun Park. The girl said she was frozen through and needed to warm up. Dunhuang agreed; the storm had blasted Beijing right back into winter. From outside, the windows of the hotpot place were blanketed in heavy steam; only shadows milled within. Inside, there was a huge crowd, all red faces and thick necks, it looked as though half of Beijing had squeezed in. Countless beer glasses were hoisted over heads, the smell of alcohol and hotpot mixed with the chatter, all rising on billowing steam. Dunhuang hadn't felt such a welcoming intimacy in months, and his heart warmed so suddenly he nearly teared up. He couldn't remember the last time he'd eaten hotpot. He loved hotpot. He remembered the first time he'd gone home for the spring festival. He had bought an electric pot with his own money, and eaten hotpot from the first of the year straight through to the sixth, when he returned to Beijing.

They picked a table in the corner, the girl seated against the wall and Dunhuang with a crowd of boisterous diners behind him. A split pot; Dunhuang liked it spicy. Three half-liter bottles of Yanjing beer. He noted that she ordered two plates of winter melon and mushrooms. The pot boiled, the mutton floated. Dunhuang lifted his glass and said, "What are we toasting?"

"Nothing. Drink your beer."

The first glass was awfully refreshing. The girl turned out not to be much of a drinker. Dunhuang could drink, he considered it his only true talent. Not many people knew it. Bao Ding thought he could hold his liquor, but once he'd gotten five shots of Erguotou in him, he never lasted to see how much Dunhuang could handle.

"You can really drink," said Dunhuang.

"You're not bad yourself."

"Nah, after one bottle I start talking nonsense."

"So go ahead, I'm listening," she said carelessly, smoothing out her sleeves. She hadn't noticed Dunhuang pouring the beer straight down his throat, hardly swallowing. "Let's drink until we talk nonsense." They started gulping beer by the half glass. Over the roiling, steaming pot, they looked like a pair of lovers. Dunhuang hadn't faced such lush temptation in months. His eyes glittered; he shoveled mutton into his mouth with his chopsticks.

"You must be starved."

"Kind of," he responded, pausing to look at his dining partner. Her face had become flushed and soft, and she appeared much younger than she had out in the wind. Not bad looking. The freckles on her nose looked pretty good. "You should eat, too."

A phone rang, and the girl quickly looked in her bag. By the time she found her phone, a man nearby had already picked his up. Her disappointment was obvious. She turned the cellphone over in her palm a few times, then put it on the table.

"What's your name?" she asked.

"Dunhuang."

"Dunhuang? That's nice. Is it your real name?"

"Of course—money back if it's not."

"Who gave it to you? Sounds pretty educated."

"My dad. Educated? He's basically illiterate; he just got lucky. My mom said that a couple days after I was born he was so frustrated by trying to pick a good name he got constipated. In the end he dragged some old newspapers over from the neighbors'. He spent a whole day looking through them, but couldn't decide on anything. Finally, he saw the headline of a *People's Daily* article about the Dunhuang Buddhist cave paintings, and that was me."

"Your dad's nuts, he should have had a name picked out before you were born!" The girl laughed emptily, her eyes flicking over her cell phone. "Guess my name."

"I don't know."

"Kuang Xia. 'Kuang' from 'spacious,' 'Xia' for 'summer.' Nice, huh?"

"That's nice. Way better than Dunhuang; I always feel like I'm some big rock they dragged out of the earth."

She laughed again, sounding more like she meant it this time, then told him that Kuang was her father's surname, and Xia was her mother's. Dunhuang didn't think it was a particularly good name. Adding your father's surname to your mother's—the world was full of people named that way. But still he said, "Nice." He felt a need to make her happy. Then he started talking about how good the DVD business was, how when he'd first come to Beijing he'd wanted to do that, but had never found an in, and regretted it ever since.

"So what do you do now?" Kuang Xia asked.

"Bit of everything. A couple days of this, a couple days of that. Beijing's too big to starve in."

"Why don't you go back home? What's so great about Beijing?"

"It's not that it's so great. It's just life, right? One place is as good as another."

Kuang Xia twirled her cellphone again, her expression growing heavy. "If I weren't selling DVDs I would have gone home ages ago. Beijing's too windy."

"It is, but the wind won't kill you."

A phone rang again, and Kuang Xia picked up the cellphone she'd just set down. Another call for someone else. Dunhuang could see something was going on, and he decided to forget it, he'd quit while he was ahead. He said, "Why don't we call it a night." Seeing how readily she agreed, he said he'd treat. He waved at a waitress to get the bill.

"I'll get it, I'll get it," she said, going for her wallet. "I said I would."

Dunhuang gestured for her to put it away, and obediently she did. He was stunned—*didn't have to twist your arm, did I?* He pretended to look for money in the pockets of his coat hanging on his seat, while a quart of sweat erupted from his body in two seconds flat. There was nothing to do but to risk a gambit Bao Ding had taught him. He rummaged around in his left pocket for a while, his forehead knotting, then rummaged in his right pocket, then he leaped to his feet and gave a panicked cry, "My wallet's gone! My cellphone, too!"

"That can't be, keep looking." Kuang Xia had stood as well.

Dunhuang went through his pockets again, then snatched up his coat and turned the two interior pockets inside out for Kuang Xia and the waitress to see. They were entirely empty, of course. "They've been stolen!" he said. "I had them when I came in." Then, to the waitress: "You've got a thief here somewhere!"

The waitress, a girl of eighteen or so, was so terrified she began to back away, as if the thief himself were bearing down on her. Her hand fluttered in negation, "We don't, we don't!" Her look of fright made Dunhuang pause, but the show, once begun, had to go on.

The chopsticks of the nearby diners all halted in mid-air, their heads turning to look with deep interest at the man who'd lost his wallet and cellphone; everyone leaned backwards slightly as if to indicate their innocence. The stage was growing larger. Dunhuang gritted his teeth and prepared his performance.

"Are you sure you didn't just put them in your bag?" asked Kuang Xia.

"Of course I'm sure. There was six hundred kuai in my wallet, maybe more. There was my bank card, my ID card, and a fifty-kuai phone card—all gone! Never mind the money, it's a huge hassle to replace an ID card. And I bought that cellphone just a few weeks ago, it cost more than a thousand."

He put on his best fussy old lady act. Practically every diner in the place was staring at him. The young waitress grew even more panicked and ran off to find the assistant manager. By the time the assistant manager arrived, Kuang Xia had noticed that the waitress had neglected the clothing cover that restaurants put over coats to thwart thieves—if she had, the wallet and phone could never have been stolen. The restaurant, therefore, bore responsibility. The manager wouldn't admit the restaurant's fault, though, he only stammered a bit as he explained that the sign on the door stated very clearly that customers should take care of their own belongings, and that the establishment wasn't responsible for any losses. Dunhuang and Kuang Xia weren't hearing any of it. If the clothing cover had been in place the restaurant would, of course, be blameless, but the fact was it wasn't in place, and who knew whether that had been intentional. The implication was clear.

"We are deeply sorry for the loss of your belongings," said the manager, finally caving. "How about we give you a 20% discount, and we'll call it even. And we'll throw in two free bottles of cold beer."

Dunhuang looked at Kuang Xia, who nodded in assent. But Dunhuang shouted, "No! We want five bottles!"

The assistant manager said, "Sir, that's the best I can do."

Dunhuang responded, "Fine, call your boss over."

The assistant manager hesitated, then left. Kuang Xia asked Dunhuang for his cellphone number: she'd call it and see if the thief was still in the restaurant. Dunhuang rattled off a number and Kuang Xia dialed, but the phone was off. It was hopeless, there was nothing else to do. *Of course,* thought Dunhuang, *there'd been no hope to begin with. That was a three-month-old number and god knows where the phone is now.* The assistant manager came back two minutes later, the waitress carrying five bottles of beer behind him. He apologized once again and said the general manager was currently engaged, but sent his apologies and agreed to give them five bottles of beer.

Dunhuang said, "All right, bag them up so she can take them home." Then to Kuang Xia: "I'm sorry, looks like this one's on you after all."

Kuang Xia said, "Never mind, it was meant to be mine to begin with." She looked at her cellphone, then suddenly stuffed it in her bag, sat down, and said to the waitress, "Open them, we'll drink them now!"

If you say so, Dunhuang thought. *No skin off my nose. It just so happens I hadn't had enough.*

They really got into it then. Kuang Xia was suddenly drinking with abandon, as though she were downing water, and they clinked their glasses with solemn determination.

"Drink, drink," she said. Two bottles later, all she could say was "drink," as she slowly slumped onto the table.

"You all right?" Dunhuang asked.

"Fine…drink. Drink." Kuang Xia spoke as if she had a fishball in her mouth, then she suddenly began to weep. "I want to go home. Take me home."

"Okay," said Dunhuang, "I'll take you home." He finished the rest of the beer straight from the bottle.

Luckily, Kuang Xia remembered the name of the place where she lived, and Dunhuang had heard of it. Three months ago, he'd known this stretch of Haidian like an old Beijinger. She lived in a one-bedroom apartment in the west section of Furongli, third floor, a rental. Dunhuang got her upstairs and opened the door to discover that the room was packed with white wicker baskets, all of them full of DVDs. Labels were stuck on the baskets: *Euro/American, Indian, Korean, Japanese,* etc. He was just thinking of looking for the baskets labeled *softcore* and *hardcore* when Kuang Xia spoke from the bed, her eyes still closed, "Water, I need water."

Dunhuang went to the kitchen, but the water cooler was empty. He ran back into the room and told her to hold on while he boiled some tapwater. While he did, she fell asleep again, rolling herself in the blanket and snoring gently. He sat down in an old wooden chair, holding the glass of water and waiting for it to cool. The room was crudely furnished; besides the queen-sized bed where Kuang Xia lay there was only one table and one chair in the whole place. On the table was an old television and a nearly-new DVD player. The rest was DVD baskets. He nosed about here and there, and ended up drinking the water himself. He couldn't imagine how he would pass the rest of the evening—where would he sleep tonight? Listening to Kuang Xia's light snores he was suddenly overcome with self-pity. He didn't have so much as a hole to crawl into. He'd been in Beijing for two years and this was the best he'd done. Thinking about it objectively, it really was too much. When he'd quit his old job in his hometown, he'd had complete faith that he could come to Beijing and make a good life—now he was the living dead. He had only twenty-two kuai and four mao in his pocket. He poured another glass of water for Kuang Xia, in case she woke up asking for a drink.

Dunhuang looked through all the baskets but found no hardcore, not even anything that could properly be considered softcore, only "romance" flicks. A woman with bared arms and legs on the cover was just a trick—he knew the whole film probably only bared that much skin. At last, he found something that sounded raunchy, a French movie called *Porno Director*. He turned on the TV and DVD player and started watching it with the sound muted. He watched half of it without seeing anything that quickened his pulse, and lost interest. His eyelids began to droop and he fell asleep in the chair. When he jerked awake the film was over, the DVD tray had ejected itself, and the TV displayed a steady deep blue with the white logo of the DVD player.

It was two thirty in the morning. He turned off the TV and DVD player, feeling cold and stiff. Kuang Xia was huddled on the other side of the bed like a cat, no longer snoring, the blanket rising and falling with her breath. *To hell with it*, Dunhuang thought, and drawing his wrinkled felt overcoat from his bag, he lay down gingerly on the queen-sized bed, curling his body up like a dog. He pulled his coat over his head and the world went dark. For him, night had come at last. He thought to scratch an itch on his chin—his hand halfway there, he slept.

3

Dunhuang's first sensation upon waking was light. When he opened his eyes, he got a shock: he was staring right into another pair of eyes, set in a lively face. His head began to clear; it was Kuang Xia, he was sleeping in her bed. He felt warm; his hand encountered a soft, fluffy blanket. He smiled, embarrassed, and began to sit up, but Kuang Xia stopped him by pressing her mouth to his. Dunhuang slowly leaned back until he was once again lying flat.

Throughout the whole process they only spoke once: Kuang Xia said, "You're on my foot."

Dunhuang was at a loss. He'd seen plenty of porn, and had practiced in his dreams, but now that he was finally doing it for real his mind had gone completely blank, and his body lay heavy and intransigent in the darkness. Kuang Xia helped him, one hand leading the way, and then she said, "You're on my foot." Dunhuang had somehow managed to step on her foot. Later, he began to understand what to do. His reason gradually returned to him. As his mind grew clearer, he was able to make use of the lessons of films and dreams. He watched as her brow knit together like cord and she clenched her teeth as if she were enduring great suffering. Her body contracted, shuddering, but apart from those few words she never made a sound.

Dunhuang rolled away from her, lightened in heart and body. He had a foolish feeling—the heavens were high and the clouds were white and the wind was blue. He had a foolish feeling that the storm had abated, that the roof of the apartment had vanished, and that the sandstorm had never visited Beijing at all.

Neither spoke. The plastic chicken alarm clock at the head of the bed ticked and tocked to itself.

"Am I pretty?" Kuang Xia asked after a long while.

"Yeah."

Silence once again.

"How old are you?" she asked.

"Twenty-five."

"Same as my younger brother," she said quietly. "I'm twenty-eight."

Dunhuang suddenly felt protective of the girl beside him, and he stammered, "Actually, I'm a…uh…I make fake ID cards."

"Oh…fake IDs. I sell pirated DVDs, we're practically colleagues."

She laughed a little. He said, "I just got out. From…inside."

He expected a cry of shock and dismay, but it didn't come. She merely repeated, in the same tone, "Oh." Then she said, "My real name is Xia Xiaorong." Dunhuang wanted to turn his head and look at her, but he stopped himself. She continued, "I made up the name 'Kuang Xia' for when I have a child."

Dunhuang felt uncomfortable, as though a sharp thread were tugging upwards from his belly and splitting open his chest. "Are you married?" he asked.

"No, and no kids yet, but my boyfriend's last name is Kuang. And mine is Xia."

Dunhuang decided he didn't want to lay there all day. He sat up and began putting on his clothes. He moved quickly, heading to the bathroom before his belt was fastened. He sat on the toilet with his pants on and smoked a cigarette. When he came out he decided to give her all of his worldly wealth and pulled from his pocket the twenty-two kuai and four mao. As he passed the little square table in the living room, he stuck the money under the ashtray. That done, he looked up and saw, through the window that separated the bedroom from the living room, Kuang Xia—whose real name was Xia Xiaorong—looking at him with her head cocked to one side.

"I want a glass of water," said Xiaorong.

Dunhuang poured a glass and brought it over. "It's hot."

Xiaorong stretched a bare arm from beneath the covers and grabbed his hand. "Do you have a girlfriend?"

All at once and for no good reason, Dunhuang felt sad. "Yeah I do!" he said. "Here in Beijing." He didn't, of course, but he thought he should say he did. As he said it, he remembered a girl Bao Ding told him about, Qibao. Bao Ding said that once he got out he should go find Qibao and take care of her. Dunhuang knew next to nothing about Qibao—he'd seen her only once, from behind. He'd arrived at Bao Ding's place just as she was leaving. She was tall and slender, with a good ass. When he mentioned her, Bao Ding laughed and said, that's Qibao. He said that she also sold fake IDs, but had told him nothing more than that. And if he wasn't telling, Dunhuang knew not to ask.

Xiaorong kept hold of his hand. "Is she pretty?" She sounded like his mother.

"She certainly wouldn't turn your stomach."

Giggling, she drew her arm in again, the blanket gently shaking with her laughter. When the laughter subsided and her body was still, she said, "When I saw you standing in the living room you looked just like my brother back home. He's a good-for-nothing, he still doesn't understand what life is. He's driving our parents crazy with worry." Then she said, "Bring her over and let me see her some time."

Now she sounded like an older sister. "I'm not exactly sure where she is," Dunhuang said.

"As long as she's in Beijing, you'll find her. Aren't you even curious why I invited you for a drink?"

Dunhuang was quiet.

"We had a fight. He said girls like me were a bore, always wanting to go home to the countryside, wanting to settle down and have kids. He said he'd rather just break up."

"You were waiting for his call."

"Yeah."

"It doesn't make a lot of sense."

"Him?"

"You."

Suddenly, she was angry: "Get out of here! It's the same bullshit with all you men!"

So he started to leave. He picked up his bag and walked out of the bedroom, but she called him back again. Her voice had softened somewhat, and she told him to look the other way while she got dressed. She only put on a shirt and then sat with the covers around her. She handed him 100 kuai. "This is all I've got," she said. "It'll have to do for now."

Wordlessly, Dunhuang took the money. As he passed through the living room he stuck the twenty-two kuai and four mao back in his pocket, too.

As far as Dunhuang was concerned, that one hour in the morning was the only good part of the day—he spent the rest of it running through Beijing's dust. The wind had dropped and dust hung in the air, neither settling nor dispersing. The people in the streets wore glasses, masks, headscarves. Carrying his bag, he first went to Xiyuan, where he and Bao Ding had rented a couple of rooms three months ago. The landlady pretended not to recognize him—after they'd been caught she'd sold what she could sell of their stuff and tossed the rest. Their rent was paid up for another month, too. Finally, Dunhuang lost his temper and cursed her, calling her a cheapskate. The landlady relented, saying he had some nerve coming back now, when the police had come asking questions—she'd lost face because of him.

"So *now* you're worried about your reputation?" Dunhuang said. "Who was it who said we should just do our thing, that it wasn't any business of yours? We were just renters!"

"Who knew you'd have the Public Security Bureau on me," she said, her tone weakening. Dunhuang heard her mutter something like, "How'd he get out so soon…"

He'd meant to just come and have a look to see if any of his stuff was left, thinking he might even rent here again. He changed his mind. "Never mind the stuff you sold, you've got to return the last month's rent. Eight hundred." Someone else had already occupied the rooms.

"Eight hundred? Where am I going to get eight hundred?" The landlady practically jumped. "I'm unemployed, my mother's ill, I've got a pile of debt…where am I going to get eight hundred?"

"Get a loan from the bank. It's not my problem."

"But I really don't have anything," she said. Suddenly, she pulled her cellphone from her pocket and started saying "Hello?" into it. She paced back and forth like Lenin, saying, "What's that? The emergency room? That serious? Okay, I'll be right there. I'll be right there!" She lowered the phone, her face sour with worry. "You see, my boy, things go bad at the drop of a hat. My mother's not well, I need to go to the hospital. I've really got nothing—why don't I give you this hundred, it's all I've got." She actually pulled an Old Man out of her pocket. "I'd be really grateful…"

Furious, Dunhuang snatched the money, it was better than nothing. The landlady turned and ran off down the alley. He watched her large ass waddling away and began to regret having taken her money. If she really was going to the emergency room, she would need everything she could get. He considered returning the money, but at the last moment remembered that she'd once told him that her parents were gone and her children grown: she had no real burdens, and the rent—well, whatever they could pay would be fine, as long as she didn't starve. Dunhuang got angry again, then realized that her cellphone hadn't seemed to ring at all, not even vibrate—that damned woman! He grabbed his bag and gave chase, but when he emerged from the alley she was nowhere in sight. He came straight back, picking up broken bricks from the base of the wall, and when he reached her place he started heaving them up onto the tiles of her roof, mumbling as he did, "one hundred, two hundred, three hundred…" As he threw the last one he yelled, "Seven hundred, and fuck you!"

After that, he went looking for a few of his old fake-ID friends. Every one of them had either moved or been caught. No surprise, the whole pack of them had been swept up at the same time. When Bao Ding had gone to jail he'd said someone had to have tipped off the police, otherwise how had they all been caught at once? He wasn't sure who it was, there were plenty of fake-ID sellers in Beijing, each with their own backers and their own territory. Those who'd been caught were beyond Dunhuang's reach, and those few who'd escaped had learned their lesson and moved their base of operations somewhere else. But Dunhuang kept up the search. He had to—he needed to get back into the game. Over the course of a whole day, he didn't see one familiar face, much less Qibao, whom he wouldn't recognize except for her back and ass: he wouldn't even know her if she introduced herself.

By nine thirty that night, Dunhuang had had only two biscuits and a bottle of water. He got off the bus at Guigumen, but he knew the minute his feet hit the pavement that he had nowhere to go. He wandered into Furongli, and saw that Xiaorong's light was on. He knocked. She cracked the door, but didn't open it. He pushed his way in.

"It's you," she said.

"I came to return your money."

She looked at him, he was covered in dust as though he'd just come from a construction site. "You struck it rich quick. Were you picking pockets or did you rob a bank?"

"I was counterfeiting money," he said, reaching into his bag. At first, he couldn't find it. He looked again, still with no success. He frowned—where was his money? "I had it right here, where could it have gone?"

"Spare me the act. Are you saying another thief got you?"

He flushed—she'd seen through him. "Last night…you knew all along?"

"Do you think I'm an idiot?" she asked. "When I called your number it wasn't off, it was out of service."

"I'm sorry," he said quickly, continuing to rummage in his bag. He found a long slash cut in the fabric and knew it was hopeless. This time he'd been robbed for real. There was no way to explain. He pulled the money Xiaorong had given him from his shirt pocket and put it on the table. "Thanks," he said, then picked up his bag and left.

When he got out of the building he suddenly felt exhausted, and sat on the steps to smoke a cigarette. The sound-activated light in the doorway eventually went out, and he sat in darkness, feeling alone and abandoned. The lights were lit in nearly every apartment above him, and the heat would still be on—they didn't know how cold the wind felt as it crept up his pant leg. They were home. He was beginning to see Xiaorong's point of view, all she wanted was a home, a husband, a child…what was wrong with that? Before he even finished the cigarette he was thinking about how someone ought to teach that bastard Kuang a lesson.

Footsteps came down the stairs behind him and Dunhuang stood up to make way. He stepped on his cigarette and headed out into the courtyard. A voice behind him said, "Stop." He looked back and Xiaorong was standing under the light in her pajamas. "Come on up."

Dunhuang felt for another cigarette.

"We'll just say the money was stolen, all right?"

"I'm not just saying it—it really was stolen."

"All right, it really was. Come on up."

Obediently, he went upstairs. As she led him up she said, "You're just as stubborn as my brother."

"How am I stubborn?" he asked.

"Stubborn's not so bad," she said, "as long as you turn out better than him." They were back in her apartment. Xiaorong went into the kitchen to make some noodles and Dunhuang told her about breaking the landlady's tiles. She giggled and said he was worse than her brother. After they finished the noodles, Dunhuang took a hot shower and changed into clean clothes. By the time he came out, she'd shut off the TV and gotten into bed.

Dunhuang asked timidly, "So did Kuang…come by?"

"He won't be coming by," she answered sternly. Silently elated, he crawled into bed and pulled back the covers to find she was crying. She stopped, but even after they started having sex she made no other sound. In the middle of it, wanting to hear her voice, Dunhuang asked through his panting, "Do you sell porn? I couldn't find any."

She replied, with difficulty, "They're under the bed."

4

When Dunhuang awoke the next morning he heard the sound of dishes in the kitchen. The thought that it was supposed to be someone named Kuang waking in his place made him sweat. Xiaorong had said his name was Kuang Shan, which meant "spacious mountain." Dunhuang's first reaction was that whoever had named him had been as lazy and empty-headed as Dunhuang's own father. They'd picked the lowest of the low-hanging fruit—but the results were kind of interesting. Xiaorong emerged from the kitchen and Dunhuang asked, "So, uh…he really isn't coming back, is he?"

"Scared?"

"My ass. Worst comes to worst I'm willing to go back to jail."

"So don't ask, then. He's dead to me."

Dunhuang bounced up from under the covers. "Okay, then he's dead to me, too!"

After breakfast, neither of them asked the other's plans. They left the house together, Xiaorong carrying a backpack full of DVDs, Dunhuang carrying all his earthly possessions. They parted in front of the Haidian gymnasium, saying nothing more than "bye."

Dunhuang spent another day wandering aimlessly, without seeing a single familiar face. Again he made it to evening on two biscuits and a bottle of water, then took the bus back to Furongli. Xiaorong opened the door for him nonchalantly, then headed to the kitchen to make noodles again. Last night there'd been one egg, tonight there were two. The dust had finally settled. Dunhuang took a quick shower, then dove underneath the bed—there really were baskets under there. He grabbed two movies with naked people on their covers.

Over the next three days, Dunhuang ate six biscuits and drank three bottles of water. Riding the public buses he traversed the city seven or eight times, and threaded through thirty or more alleyways, but he finally despaired. He couldn't find his people, no possible comeback presented itself. He carried his pack back to Furongli, and when Xiaorong opened the door she said, "You're back. Why don't you take a break tomorrow—if you want to, you can come sell DVDs with me."

The next morning they left the house together; Xiaorong was empty-handed, Dunhuang had a pack full of movies. Dunhuang was in excellent spirits as they passed the east gate of Peking University, and said to Xiaorong, "Here I am, a vocational school graduate, reduced to selling DVDs. If I hadn't been so lazy, not even Qinghua or Peking University could have denied me."

"So why don't you stop selling DVDs," she countered. "The doors of PU are still open."

"Nope, can't give it up," said Dunhuang. "A man's got to eat."

"But I thought you could get by just fine as 'vocational school graduate,'" said Xiaorong.

"If that were the case," he answered, "I'd have been getting by just fine for years."

That morning, they set up on a street in Xiyuan. They laid a few dozen movies out by the entrance of a busy supermarket. Xiaorong's bag was multipurpose; unzipped and laid flat it was an ideal display case. Xiaorong knew her DVDs backwards and forwards, and when anyone mentioned a title she knew, she fished it out of the pile immediately. But if they made special requests, she was at a loss. She could elaborate at length on the ones she'd seen, but past that she was helpless. If anyone happened to ask for Hong Kong action or martial arts flicks Dunhuang stepped in. In middle school and high school he'd spent all his spare time in a run-down film shop, where, in his boredom, he'd seen practically everything Jackie Chan, Chow Yun-fat, and Steven Chow had made. He also knew how to chat up customers better than Xiaorong. And no wonder—his old job selling fake IDs had relied almost entirely on banter.

In the afternoon, they went to the gate of the Agricultural University. He often came here selling IDs, and knew the area well; students needed fake IDs just like the rest of society. When it came time for the job hunt, in particular, they showed up in droves wanting fake transcripts and certificates of honor, the gutsy ones even asking for fake diplomas or degrees: polytech students wanting to be BAs, BAs wanting to be MAs, MAs wanting to be PhDs. It went the other way, too: older doctoral students wanting undergraduate student IDs for the half-price tickets to public parks. The students were enthusiastic consumers of movies, too. Xiaorong said they were all film buffs, going straight for the art-house and classics—the older the film the better it sold. It was something Dunhuang didn't get. Just watching a black and white movie made him dizzy. That stuff was beyond him.

That day, at any rate, Dunhuang talked up a hurricane with the customers, and they did well. Xiaorong said she never would have guessed. Dunhuang said selling fake IDs was all talk, just a matter of convincing people that fakes were better than the real thing. It was just like fortune telling.

"All right then," she replied, "I'll hire you as my Secretary of DVD Sales."

"No problem," he said, "I'll serve you faithfully, even in bed." Xiaorong's face darkened and Dunhuang knew he'd gone too far. He acted like a contrite elementary school student, but thought, *Isn't that what this is? I serve you, and you serve me?*

All in all, though, Dunhuang made an excellent secretary. He counted the cash, drummed up business, shilled in the crowd, and served as bodyguard and footman. Most importantly, he was able—under normal circumstances—to turn Xiaorong's bad moods into good moods, and make her good moods even better. "Abnormal circumstances" were those that involved Kuang Shan. If her attention happened to wander as they spoke, Dunhuang looked around for lovers holding hands, or new parents out for a stroll with their babies. *It's better this way,* thought Dunhuang. *It keeps me from getting in too deep.* But it also made him want to smoke. As he drew deep lungfuls and coughed, he'd tell himself again: *it's better this way.*

To perfect his sales tactics, Dunhuang began watching arthouse cinema in quantity—he needed to cram. He often fell asleep as he watched, however, and in his dreams the films became blockbusters, romances, action, horror, and, of course, porn. He couldn't understand why Xiaorong never sold the porn under her bed. She told him Kuang Shan used to sell those, she didn't like talking about them, and didn't like selling them.

"There's nothing wrong with them," Dunhuang said, as they

ate noodles in her apartment. "The working classes need it."

"What do you know about the working classes? It's you who needs it."

"I do, and so do the working classes. 'We must emerge from the masses, and return to the masses.' Look how well the older ladies do. Even with kids on their backs they keep class sentiment in mind, always asking everyone, 'Hey there comrade, want a DVD? They're stimulating!'"

His impression set her to giggling, but then she got annoyed again. "I see, so to you I'm just some 'older lady'? Prowling around with a kid on my back?"

"No!" he said. "You've got those old ladies beat. Our Comrade Xia Xiaorong boasts both youth and beauty, and has sworn to sell only art films."

She rolled her eyes at him. "I'm old, I know it, and I never even graduated from high school. I can't compare to you, a voc-tech student who turns his nose up at Peking University."

"See?" he said, laughing. "Art-film lovers can't stand to hear the truth. What's wrong with me saying you're young, beautiful, graceful, and refined?"

"A whole bowl of noodles can't shut you up," she said. "Do the dishes!"

He went to wash the dishes, but at the sink his mind wandered back to the porn. It was harder to sell than the usual movies, because you couldn't just lay it out in the open, but the price was almost twice as high, and that was pure profit. His empty wallet was making him nervous, he wanted to make money, he couldn't keep living out of someone else's pocket. He hadn't come to Beijing just to be a burden. He'd had a realization a few days ago, as he was passing Haidian bridge and thinking of Bao Ding in jail.

Bao Ding was five years older than him, and had been in

Beijing for five years. He was big and powerful, built to lead a gang, so Dunhuang had thrown in with him. Back home, Dunhuang had heard about the low cost and high profit of making fake IDs—you just talked the talk, then waited for people to hand over cash. And it was more or less true. After following Bao Ding around for a couple of weeks he had grasped the basics. Bao Ding and Dunhuang were at the lowest level of the operation—bringing in the business. If they saw someone looking around expectantly they sidled over and asked, "Need an ID? We've got everything, even a passport's no problem." Then they discussed price, took an advance, and found someone to make what the customer needed. They weren't involved in the actual making of the documents, they just negotiated the price and exchanged the cash and goods. They got a share of the proceeds strictly according to the work they brought in; the more deals they closed, the more they made. If, in the course of things, they ran across a big spender, then it was like Christmas, and the good life seemed nearly within reach. There was another similarity between selling IDs and selling DVDs, besides the fact that they were all fake—you needed to know your product. You had to know what a bachelor degree diploma looked like, all the different kinds of parking permits, what was usually in a personal document folder, and so on. You needed to be able to stand by your work, and that took experience, trustworthiness, and clear standards. None of that was a problem for Dunhuang, who soon knew the profession inside and out. The real problem was the unexpected, which usually meant the police. When you saw the police you needed to make a quick decision whether you were going to keep your head down or make a break for it; whether you'd hide the IDs on your person or toss them. If caught, different actions led to different degrees of punishment. All that took experience.

That's where Dunhuang went wrong. On that day, he'd gone with Bao Ding to the overpass by Pacific Computer City. It was a deal he'd arranged himself and he had the document on him, a master's diploma. The deal was supposed to take place at a quarter past nine that morning, and they arrived at ten after. They waited until nine thirty without seeing the customer, and just as they were about to leave they saw two policemen strolling in their direction. Bao Ding said, very quietly, "Careful." Just then, the policemen broke into a run, and Bao Ding shouted, "Go!" The police were coming straight for them. Dunhuang ran after Bao Ding, passing the south gate of Peking University and heading for Haidian. As they ran, Bao Ding told Dunhuang to ditch the diploma. With no evidence, they'd just get a beating and then be released, but if they were caught red-handed there would be trouble. Dunhuang, confident they'd escape, refused, and his confidence infected Bao Ding. The police officers behind them weren't in the least bit worrisome, they were so fat they practically had to hold their bellies as they ran. They weren't quite able to shake them, but there was no way they'd get caught. They headed south, away from the electronics stores, hoping to get past the bridge and into Book City, where there were lots of people and lots of doors, and where they'd be harder to catch than rats.

Luck wasn't with them, however, and as they passed Haidian Bridge they saw a police car and four officers on the street. Looking back, they found the two pigs had gained on them. Bao Ding knew it was serious, and told Dunhuang to hurry up and toss the document. Dunhuang, who'd never been caught in a police cordon before, ran with the diploma in his hand, not knowing how to get rid of it. Bao Ding snatched it from him, and he'd just tossed it when they were surrounded by the police. They'd all seen him do it, and one of them fished it out of the garbage can.

"Whose is this?" he asked.

Bao Ding glanced at Dunhuang and said, "Mine."

The officer asked Dunhuang, "Is it really his?"

"Yes," said Dunhuang.

Later, Dunhuang consoled himself that Bao Ding had shrugged his right shoulder twice, a signal they'd arranged for when they were negotiating with a customer. It meant: *follow my lead*. So, Dunhuang followed Bao Ding's lead, right up until he finally got out of jail, three months later. That diploma meant that Bao Ding would be sent somewhere farther away, who knew for how long. When Dunhuang was released, Bao Ding's trial hadn't even begun.

As Dunhuang and Xiaorong passed Haidian Bridge, Dunhuang resolved to make some money and buy Bao Ding's freedom. When you got down to it, Bao Ding had taken the fall for Dunhuang. And during their two years together in Beijing he'd taken good care of Dunhuang. Everyone in their business knew: it was better to stay out of jail, of course, but if you went in it wasn't cause for despair. What went in had to come out. As long as you could find the right contacts, grease the right palms, your problems could be solved. It didn't matter that Bao Ding's trial hadn't begun, and even if he had already been sentenced Dunhuang could still get him out with the right payoffs. But it would take money, Dunhuang thought. *Money...* Dunhuang and Xiaorong lay in bed that night, covered in sweat but unwilling to move, both too lazy to get up and turn off the porn they'd put on. Eventually, they played rock-paper-scissors, and Dunhuang lost. Naked, he shut off the TV and DVD player, and as he stood with the disc stuck on his finger, about to put it back in its case, he stopped and said to Xiaorong, "I want to sell porn."

"Are you crazy?" she said. "If they catch you there'll be hell to pay."

"I need money to get Bao Ding out."

Xiaorong had been going to say that she had plenty of money, but when she heard what it was for she kept quiet. She'd saved up over the years, but she meant to use it for going back home and getting married, buying a house, and raising a child. She'd planned it for years. Kuang Shan had once nursed designs on that nest egg, but she'd batted him away, swearing that barring some disaster like her parents falling ill, no one would touch the money. Obviously, she wouldn't volunteer it to ransom Bao Ding, and she wouldn't be coerced, either—her mind was made up. She was also quite aware that her meager savings might not be enough. Dunhuang had once told her that you couldn't even start a conversation without twenty or thirty thousand. Xiaorong kept quiet.

"So, I'm thinking," Dunhuang put away the DVD and lay down on his side, holding Xiaorong. "I'll help you sell the porn, they're just going to waste as is. If you're embarrassed by it…" Dunhuang paused, staring at Xiaorong's ear, feeling his courage coming, "I don't need to follow you. I'll go off and sell them by myself."

"That's what this is really about, isn't it?" she asked.

"Don't get me wrong, I just want to earn enough to get Bao Ding out as soon as possible. I'm not trying to skin you."

"I didn't mean that," said Xiaorong, turning her back to him. "I was just wondering why men are all like that, always insisting on striking out, going it alone, always leaving the girl behind."

"We're not leaving you behind, we're worried you'll get

hurt. What's wrong with staying out of the action? Men aren't gods, we can't keep track of everything."

"Whatever," she said after a while. "Take a few other movies along and sell them at the same time. Just give me what they cost."

Dunhuang was elated, and held her closer. What a great girl she was, so considerate of others. At last he could make his own money.

5

Dunhuang picked out three hundred kuai worth of DVDs. He'd worked it out—if he sold them all he'd clear five hundred in profit, even more if he could bump up the price on the porn. Instantly, he felt as refreshed as if he'd just stepped out of a bath. There wasn't a cloud in the sky and good times were right around the corner. That wasn't how he'd felt the first time he'd split from Bao Ding to pull ID business on his own. Then he'd been panicked, reticent, out of his depth—what he was doing was illegal, after all. It was different now, though. He was an old hand, calloused, nonchalant. Anyway, selling pirated DVDs was miles closer to legality than making fake IDs. And what was most important was his return to entre-preneurship—he was basically restarting his life in Beijing. He reminded himself constantly that he was working for himself, and that filled him with confidence.

Every morning, he and Xiaorong left Furongli together, then went their separate ways. Dunhuang had a plan—he couldn't keep selling piecemeal like they had been. Guerrilla sales would never bring in much, and it was exhausting to always be on the run. It would be better to find a set location and build up regular clientele. He'd thought it through. There were only three types of clients. One was students, who spent money without batting an eyelash—they wanted art. Next was office drones, the kind of people that flipped through newspapers while clipping their nails—they wanted entertainment. The more educated office workers even more so. Thinking people tended to feel dissatisfied with life and they watched movies for distraction. Movies were just as good as cuddling your husband or wife, and more dignified. Third were white collar workers and company managers—too busy to even take a piss, they needed relaxation more than anyone. To splay out on the sofa and enjoy a good story. Not a book—who still read books?—but a film, a feature film, a big Hollywood blockbuster. If only Spielberg made a new movie every week...

The problem was how to get in touch with these types of people and build long-term relationships—unloading some high-price porn in the process. It would take a little time, of course, before things took off—earning money took patience. Dunhuang knew all about that.

Dunhuang spent the day thinking about how to make more money. He did some business, too, opening his bag outside a supermarket. The advantage there was that everyone who came out had change in their pocket, and didn't mind spending it. Most of them were housewives, looking for an escape from their tedious housework. They liked romances, preferably tear-jerkers, so when Dunhuang saw them coming he took out the DVDs with pictures of men and women embracing on the sleeves. Then he'd start his spiel. "This story will sweep you off your feet." "You'll use up two jumbo rolls of paper towels mopping up the tears." "This one's so sad it could drive you to off yourself." "Watching this one could move a couple to patch up a divorce, let alone a mere lover's quarrel." If that didn't do the trick, Dunhuang laid it on even thicker: "The newspapers say this film is perfect for both working women and housewives. It's the chicken soup of love, the Bible of the heart. Whether it's problems in your love life or disharmony in your home, this movie is just the thing. You can throw away your standard dictionary of Chinese characters, but you can't miss this film. It goes beyond the mere definition of *film*." Dunhuang dredged up every cliché he'd ever heard, relevant or not. He'd succeeded once they pulled out their wallets. The women were easy to handle as long as you were willing to talk as though love was the be-all and end-all.

The men around the supermarket entrance were, by comparison, tight-fisted. They always acted like successful businessmen, with no time for pirated films. Really, Dunhuang knew, they were just embarrassed. If there was no one else around, they'd look over the DVDs with the more provocative covers, zeroing in on disheveled heroines so unerringly that you'd think they had infrared guidance systems. Male customers required handling, they had to be led along gently. In such cases, Dunhuang spoke first, "Hello, sir. These are all new releases, take a look. I've got everything."

If they approached, Dunhuang would say—as if to himself, but loud enough for the man to hear, "The American and European ones aren't all that. It's the Korean and Japanese that are really good. Clean, attractive."

The man would be careful to feign ignorance, nonchalantly saying "Got any? Let's have a look."

"Would you like something heavy on story, or heavy on naturalism?"

"What's that mean?" they'd ask, as though it were all the same to them.

"Well, the ones with story don't really hold up over time," he'd say. "Who wants to watch the same story over and over?

The ones that emphasize naturalism…those are different. They're closer to real life, as if they know you better than you know yourself, and every time you re-watch them you'll be rewarded with something new. You can watch a good movie a hundred times. It's just like something they'd say in the paper: 'These movies are in line with human nature, they're actually beneficial to the mental and physical health of the modern man.'" He elevated the porn to a moral and ethical level, trying to ease the men's embarrassment. Just think, if porn was on par with the "construction of a spiritual civilization," what was there to be shy about?

"You sure can talk!" they'd say as they glanced around casually, unwilling to commit themselves. "Show me a couple."

Dunhuang would pull a few DVDs from the interior pocket of his bag and give the men a glimpse of the covers, saying, "Guaranteed high quality, if you've got complaints you can bring them straight back to me." They'd lean over to look, pull out one or two movies that caught their eye, and then say:

"I'll give these a try. How much?"

"Fifteen." When their expressions changed, he'd quickly add, "High-quality stuff is hard to find. Honestly, there are only a few places in the whole city where you can get it. You might be able to buy something for three kuai elsewhere, but it won't be like what I've got. Just try it out. Quality is the key— we have to ask ourselves, is it truly and honestly beneficial to our mental and physical health?"

"Truly and honestly" would get them. Most of the men who stopped to take a look would buy a DVD or two. And they did so with a clear conscience, without a blush on their face, without their pulse racing. Perfect. These movies were three times as profitable as the normal ones.

When he packed up that first evening, Dunhuang calculated

that he'd made 120 kuai in profit, a rousing day of business. The first time he'd drawn in fake-ID business on his own, he'd only made eighty. He was thrilled, and he bought half a kilo of the duck necks Xiaorong liked, a half-rack of beer, and an order of oil-poached fish to go. He returned jubilantly to Furongli to celebrate the beginning of his independent DVD-selling career with Xiaorong. He rode high on his good mood, drinking four bottles of beer to Xiaorong's one, and was thirsty for more. She told him to slow down, worried what might happen if he drank too much. Dunhuang, careless in his cheerfulness, said, "What's another four bottles?"

Xiaorong tilted her head and glared at him as she chewed a duck neck.

"Honest to god, besides a full bladder, beer's got no effect on me."

She thumped her duck neck onto the table. "Honest to *nothing*. You tricked me! You stayed at my house that night because you were pretending to be drunk!"

Dunhuang's glass, halfway to his lips, lowered to the table. He'd forgotten that he used that little ruse. How did girls have such good memories? "I didn't trick you," he said, "I had just gotten out of jail that day, I was out of practice, I really was tipsy. Sure, it was a little bit tricky, but I wouldn't have dared to stay otherwise. It was because I liked you."

"Oh, thanks very much! Who needs it?"

But she was slightly mollified, and Dunhuang was secretly pleased with himself. Ha, people were all too vain to withstand love. He picked up another duck neck and passed it to her. "I didn't just like you," he continued, clinking his glass against hers. "It was love at first sight."

She retrieved the duck neck, amenable, and dropped her

head to chew on it absently. But he heard her mutter: "You can forget about love at first sight."

Dunhuang was as pleased as a duck who'd escaped the knife, and said, "A toast to us!"

Dunhuang's DVDs sold well, and he earned more than Xiaorong nearly every day. He didn't forget about her, though, he offered to raise her return an extra five mao. She rejected the offer, but he did it anyway. In addition, he always made sure to bring home some buns or biscuits or vegetables in the evening. He'd tell her he just happened to pick them up, but secretly he still worried about being a burden on her. He didn't know when their arrangement might suddenly change—it was the worst, relying on an uncertain relationship for uncertain lodgings. The fifth day after he struck out on his own, Dunhuang used his earnings to buy a second-hand Nokia. He called Xiaorong and disguised his voice, asking, "Are you acquainted with a man named Dunhuang?" Xiaorong said, "Who is this? What do you want him for?"

"This is the police station, we suspect him of selling pornographic videos, and he's currently in detention," he answered. Xiaorong made a noise of dismay, her voice rising as she asked, "Where is he? You tell me where he is right now!" Dunhuang couldn't help bursting into laughter. Xiaorong was silent for a moment, then caught on. "You…is this you, Dunhuang?"

"Of course! I got myself a cell phone!"

Xiaorong was so angry she swore at him. "Go to hell!" and then hung up. Dunhuang was still laughing cheerfully. He sent her a text, *Damn it's nice to know someone's looking out for you! Even going back to jail would be worth it.* She sent back, *In your dreams! Who's looking out for you? You don't even look out for yourself!* Dunhuang felt happy anyway, and for the rest of the day he went around grinning, somewhat disconcertingly, at people he didn't even know.

The cell phone was soon put to use. While he was selling DVDs outside the south gate of Peking University, two students asked if he had *Run Lola Run*. He went through his bag and, sure enough, found a copy. He'd never seen the movie, but had stuck it in his bag because of the red-haired girl running on the cover—he just liked how it looked. One of the students said, "Thank god, we've finally found a copy. Good movies are damned hard to find."

A light went on in Dunhuang's head, and he asked, "So that's a good movie?"

The other student answered, "Of course, it's a classic. We looked through all the DVD shops in the neighborhood and couldn't find it. Do you have any more copies? Our whole class needs to watch it, the professor assigned a critique."

"How many copies?"

"Twenty or thirty, at least, what do you think?" one said to the other.

"That should do it."

Dunhuang's heart leaped in his throat. *I'll be damned, that's some cash.* He quickly asked if tomorrow was too late, he could bring them over. The students said that was fine, the sooner the better, they would buy them for the other students. They exchanged phone numbers, and the students said they'd contact him after class the next day. Dunhuang called Xiaorong, who happened to be near their re-supply shop, and when she came home that night she brought back thirty copies of *Run Lola Run*. The next day the two students called him, and, sure enough, they bought all thirty.

Thirty in one stroke. Dunhuang was thrilled. It was like before, when he'd get a whole pile of fake ID orders at once. As the students were walking away he ran after them, saying they should call him if they needed more DVDs in the future. As long as he had it in stock, he'd deliver right away. He was afraid they'd lose his number, so he wrote it down on two pieces of paper and gave one to each of them.

Later on, the two students—one was named Huang, the other Zhang—really did call him with orders. First it was *Der Himmel über Berlin*, then two different versions of *Spring in a Small Town*: Fei Mu's original version, and the Tian Zhuangzhuang remake. They had all been assigned as subjects for critiques, and between the three films he sold a total of ninety-eight copies.

6

Their living arrangement came to an end after twenty-one days. That evening was no different than any other, except for a high wind. High winds are nothing special in Beijing—it's a rare day when the branches *aren't* tossing. But it was really blowing that night. It sounded like a crowd of children was weeping outside the window. There was something wrong with Xiaorong's windows, they rattled heavily, as if the crowd of children wasn't just weeping, but pounding on the glass, too. Xiaorong was tucked into bed by ten past eleven, flipping through an old magazine. Her phone beeped to indicate an incoming message, and when she looked at it, her expression became complicated. When Dunhuang emerged from the bathroom she was still bent over the phone, scanning the message over and over, but not actually reading it at all. Instead, she was waiting for Dunhuang.

Dunhuang was wrapped in a towel, and nothing else. He didn't see the point, he'd just have to undress again for bed. When he entered the bedroom Xiaorong said, "He's coming." Dunhuang unwrapped his towel and said, "That's right he's coming. And here he is."

Xiaorong waved the phone at him. "He's coming over

around midnight." Seeing Dunhuang's stunned look, she added quietly, "He's coming to apologize."

Dunhuang felt coolness on his lower body as the towel began sliding all the way off. He grabbed hold of it and re-wrapped himself. He understood. Xiaorong's head hung low and he couldn't see her expression behind her bangs. He turned slowly and retrieved his clothes from the back of the chair—his underwear, shirt, sweater, long underwear, and jeans, and his socks and shoes from the floor. Holding his clothes, he went into the bathroom to get dressed. The heat of the shower hadn't dispersed, but as he dressed he felt goose bumps rising on his upper arms. When he was done, he folded the towel and put it neatly away and collected his toothbrush, toothpaste, shaving cream, and razor before coming out. He put these things into a shopping bag with a few other small items, then stuffed that bag into the backpack he'd carried the first time he came into the apartment. He discovered that, after only a few short days, he'd somehow accumulated too much stuff to fit in the pack. No matter how simple and trivial life was, it still swelled up on you, expanding pointlessly. In the past, he'd only very occasionally had the sense that his life might be superfluous. But now—as if he was perched out at the very edge of the world, as if he were a hateful tumor hanging peril-ously from the side of life—it abruptly seemed that absolutely everything about him was unnecessary. He found the largest Carrefour shopping bag in the house and determined to col-lect his pointless belongings. Once he was done, he would make himself scarce before the other guy came. It was only right. Everything in order, he hoisted his pack, picked up the shopping bag, and made to leave. Xiaorong finally spoke.

"Take the DVDs with you."

He said nothing, and continued toward the door. She

jumped out of bed and dragged him back by the strap of his pack. He turned and saw her bare legs—in fact her whole lower body was bare, the patch of fur dark at her crotch. Unashamed, Xiaorong took his hand and placed it on her bare thigh, then slid it upwards and inwards. Dunhuang felt the hair, curly, smooth, clean, and gleaming brightly.

"We've been together ten years," she murmured, her other hand feeling for Dunhuang's jacket zipper, pulling it gently up and down. She liked the sound zippers made. "All I want now is to go back home, to have a family. I want my own house and my own child. I don't want to stay here any longer."

Dunhuang smiled at her and said, "You should go back." His hand was still on her skin; she had goose bumps from the cold. The weather forecast had said that another sandstorm was on the way, the temperature was dropping. Perhaps winter would return tomorrow.

"Take the DVDs," she said again. "Call me when they're sold and I'll bring you some more."

He thought about it, and said okay. He removed his hand and took the bag. Some were regular DVDs, some were porn. He went out the door laden with his three bags, like a traveler setting out on a long journey. As he left he finally saw her tears fall.

The wind outside was so brutal it nearly tipped him over. He considered looking up to see if Xiaorong was watching from the window, but checked himself in the act. Lowering his gaze, he went out the compound gate into the teeth of the wind. His hair wasn't completely dry, and the wind felt like cold water splashed on his head. He wanted a cigarette. A few days ago, Xiaorong had forbidden him from smoking after he brushed his teeth in the evening. He hadn't understood the logic. Now it felt as though several days' worth of cravings were hitting him all at once. He broke into a run beneath the stuttering streetlamp and found a wall that blocked the wind where he could light up. He tossed his bags down and slumped to the ground. After chain-smoking five cigarettes the pack was empty, but he wanted more. It was past midnight. He stood up, dusting off his chilled butt, and went to buy another pack.

Hardly anyone was on the street, the few people he saw were closed up in their cars, passing through the wind like strange and lonely spirits. The supermarkets and corner stores were all closed, and Beijing's lively nightlife had been canceled on account of the wind. He would have to find a 24-hour mart. He couldn't for the life of him think of one nearby. He'd been in Beijing for two years and thought he knew Haidian like the back of his hand, but the moment the sun went down it was someplace else entirely. It didn't mean squat to know a place in the daytime, that was just seeing. To really know a place means knowing it at night. Now it was night, and Dunhuang's eyes were veiled in darkness, darker than Beijing itself. He followed the street, the big pack on his back and a smaller bag in each hand, deciding he would follow the street until it brought him to a brightly-lit minimart.

He finally found it at one thirty in the morning, and bought two packs of Zhongnanhais. In a windless corner he quickly smoked six in a row, and afterwards felt cold, worn-out, and sleepy. It was two in the morning. Dunhuang started to think about finding a place for the night. Most of the hotels would already be closed, and he couldn't think of any cheap ones nearby, anyway. He just needed a place to crash, anything would do, just a place where he could pay for a bunk. He thought it over, but his eyes were still masked by darkness. He felt like a failure. This was Beijing: you could spend your whole life kicking around the place and still not know what was right outside your door. Given that he didn't know how much a night's lodging would cost (only half a night, now), and given how little he had in his pocket, he decided to forget about finding a hotel. He'd just stay awake as long as he could—the sun had to come up eventually.

He wandered in fits and starts through the wind, the sand continually blowing into his mouth. On a night like this, he'd have to pass the time in whatever strange manner he could. He looked at the wind in the trees, looked at the ground, the buildings, the signs, everything that presented itself to his gaze. He discovered that, as the wind blew past the branches, ground, and buildings, it seemed to be torn to shreds, quite unlike the wind in his old village, which moved slowly over the fields like water. Beijing's wind was black and cold, while the wind at home was light yellow and warm. He smoked and the taste mixed with the sand, leaving his mouth dry and numb. He walked slowly, and by three thirty he was as stiff and unfeeling as a piece of wood—a frozen board. His body seemed to be getting lighter, a grubby lightness. If it weren't for the three bags weighing him down the wind would have blown him away. All he wanted now was a place to lie down, even just for five minutes. He'd wandered into an area he didn't recognize at all. In front of him was a crudely-built breakfast hut slumped on the sidewalk in front of a shop entrance, its eaves unusually long. Dunhuang thought he might be able to lie down under those eaves.

The windows and doors of the hut were shut tight, and with the streetlights behind him it was hard to make out anything inside, but he had a general sense of its empty darkness. From the look of it, it had been abandoned for some time— otherwise it wouldn't be leaning the way it did. Dunhuang pushed at the door and window but they were shut tight. He considered finding a brick and breaking the glass—at least he'd be out of the wind. This damned weather, it wouldn't be nearly as bad if not for the wind. He couldn't find a brick and was just about to use his elbow when a car turned a corner nearby, its headlights sweeping over the galvanized steel roll-door and the windows of the shop. The light reflected onto the breakfast hut, and Dunhuang saw a small hole in its window. He stuck a finger inside, found the latch, gave a tug, and the window opened.

Breakfast had once been sold through this window, and it was just big enough for him to push the three bags inside, then crawl in after them. The hut was filled with the choking smell of dust—it had to have been abandoned for six months at least. As his eyes gradually grew accustomed to the darkness, he found a pile of old newspapers in the corner and realized that someone must have stayed here before. Maybe someone like him, who needed a place to sleep. It made plenty of sense. Whoever it was had probably made that little hole in the window.

He spread the newspapers out and put his wool coat on top, then lay down and covered himself with clothes from his bag. The wind was kept outside, only negligible puffs found their way through the cracks. Dunhuang felt a warmth he'd never felt before. The guy who'd slept there before had the right idea, and Dunhuang felt a quiet camaraderie with him. Was the guy truly homeless or, like him, someone who had suddenly found himself with nowhere to go? Or perhaps it was a girl who'd simply gotten lost. There was no way to know, but he was certain of one thing: whoever it was had slept here overnight, possibly two or more nights. Dunhuang was highly satisfied with his conclusion. He chuckled in the darkness, then lay his head back and slept.

It was a good night's sleep, without so much as a single dream. He opened his eyes to a world of light. It was a bright, sunny day, and the sounds of cars and people were pouring in. Beijing had been restored to its usual lively racket. Dunhuang sat up and moved his mouth, it felt as if he'd spent the night eating dust, and he spat repeatedly before feeling better. Everything in the hut was coated with a thick layer of dust, far more than he'd imagined the night before. When he felt sufficiently awake, he stood up and pulled open the window. Pedestrians passed by occasionally, and a few steps away a middle-aged lady was selling fried crepes. The wind had stopped, and the world held nothing that could stop him. The leisurely pedestrians turned their heads to watch a young man passing bags out of a breakfast hut. Dunhuang ignored them, climbing out after his bags. As he swatted the dust from his body he smelled the crepes, and suddenly felt starved and thirsty. He went to the lady's stall and said,

"One crepe and a cup of soy milk."

The middle-aged lady smiled at him and started his crepe. Dunhuang reached out and picked up a cup of soy milk with plastic film over the top, stuck a straw through the film, and started drinking. By the time he was done the crepe was ready, and the lady had cracked an egg on top.

"How much?" he asked, the crepe already in his mouth, so hot it made him jump.

"It's free," the lady answered. "Go ahead."

Dunhuang's brain short-circuited for a moment, then he understood. He hurled the crepe on the ground, then pulled ten kuai from his pocket, slapped it on her stall, and said, "I'm not a fucking beggar! I don't need your pity!" He snatched up his bags and left, not even turning his head as the lady cried "Hey, your money!" behind him. Holding his back stiffly upright, he strode awkwardly, like a tragic monster. As people passed him they turned their heads for another look, curious about the young man with tears streaming down his face. Dunhuang ignored them and continued straight on until he came to a round traffic mirror at a curve in the street. In the mirror he saw a completely unfamiliar person. His head and face were coated in dust, his medium-length hair a grayish-white, and there were two clean tracks left by his tears. Basically, he was a clown. His jacket hung askew on his body, the left side higher than the right, his round-collared sweater was misshapen and bulging. His pants were horribly wrinkled, and from the look of his shoes he appeared to have just crossed a desert. What could he be but a tramp? What could he be but a beggar? Even his three bags were ugly as sin. Dunhuang wiped his face and turned around. The middle-aged lady's head was bent forward as she made crepes for someone else.

"Ma'am."

She looked up at him, then back down at her crepes, as though she hadn't seen him.

"Ma'am, I'm sorry." Dunhuang ducked his head in apology. "Please don't be angry. I'd like to buy another crepe and a cup of soy milk."

"Wait until I'm done with this one," she answered. "You're a hot-tempered guy."

Dunhuang grinned bashfully, and apologized again.

Two crepes and two cups of soy milk came to eight kuai; she gave him two kuai change. She told him she'd felt sorry for him, the way he looked—it was hard being away from home. Dunhuang lied, saying he'd only gotten off the train the night before, when it had been too late to find a hotel. She began dispensing hackneyed advice with relish, saying things like "home is mother, on the road there's no other," and how he should watch out for bad people. Seeing that she was picking up steam, Dunhuang quickly excused himself and left.

The problem now was where to stay. He couldn't afford rent—Beijing's landlords were all penny pinchers, wanting three months, six months, or even a year's rent in advance. Short of selling his body, he had no way to produce three months' rent. He needed to find a place he could rent by the day or the week, preferably a bed in a dorm, four or more to a room—the more people, the cheaper the rent. Dunhuang headed toward Peking University. Three Corners, in the center of campus, was blanketed with ads for places like that.

A basement in Chengzeyuan, near Peking University, four beds, 25 kuai per bed per night. Dunhuang contacted the landlord and asked to see the place, and the landlord arranged to meet him at the west gate of PU. He arrived a half-hour later, a thin, sickly-looking man in his forties, his back a little bent. Last night's wind could have launched him into the sky without much trouble. They passed through Yuxiuyuan and crossed the bridge to Chengzeyuan. Dunhuang had been to the building a year ago, delivering goods. There was an old intertwining willow in the yard, it's belly rotten hollow, big enough to crawl inside.

The basement room was small, with a dank chill, and laid out like a cramped student dorm. Two bunk beds nearly filled the place, and a small table and basin stand took up the rest. Odds and ends covered the table, and the basin was full of towels and toothbrushes and whatnot. Three of the beds were already occupied, only one upper bunk was empty. Bags were shoved under the beds. The landlord said the other three were all auditing classes at Peking University, planning to apply for master's programs, and they were guaranteed to be safe and reliable roommates. Dunhuang had a bad feeling about the place, though—it reminded him of something you'd see in a horror movie. He wasn't serious about staying, so he made a casual counter-offer.

"How about 20?"

"How long are you staying?"

"Won't be long. A week."

"All right then," the landlord agreed swiftly, then added in a conspiratorial tone, "When the other three come back don't tell them you're paying 20, they all pay 25."

Dunhuang considered, and decided to stay. It was better than the breakfast hut. "All right. I'll say I'm paying 30."

The landlord laughed, but even his laughter was sick, tinged a hollow and choleric red.

7

So he found himself living on a top bunk. After he put away his things, Dunhuang went to take a shower in the washroom, which was barely big enough to turn around in. Scrubbed and proper, he shouldered his bag and went out onto the street. He ate noodles and planned where he'd go to sell the rest of his DVDs; he couldn't let the morning go to waste. He'd go to Peking University and set up in the street-side flea market outside building 32.

The market had started as a perfectly ordinary stretch of street, a place where graduating students sold their old books and supplies at the end of the year. Then it slowly became an on-campus flea market, where minor trade took place year-round. By the time dusk fell, Dunhuang had gotten rid of eleven DVDs, one of them in exchange for books. The next vendor over was selling used books and the two of them chatted idly all afternoon, and when customers were scarce they pawed through each other's goods. Dunhuang picked up a book on film criticism and saw it contained a whole essay on *Run Lola Run*. He glanced through it, and found himself drawn in, thinking the author made some good points. After selling 31 copies of the movie, he'd finally gotten curious, and steeled himself to watch it. He honestly didn't like it, he couldn't figure out what the director and that constantly-sprinting Lola were trying to express. The essay, however, explained it all perfectly, sweeping away the confusions that had cluttered his mind. He bit his nails as he read.

"Fuck," said Dunhuang to the guy selling books. "Who'd have thought it was such a deep film." He continued flipping through the book, muttering as he did, "Not bad…not bad…" He thought the book was good, in part, simply because he could understand it. He'd always assumed academic writing was lofty and profound, and a real bitch to get through. This was exciting—he practically felt like an intellectual.

"If it's good, buy it," said the guy. "We're buddies, I'll give you half off." It cost twenty.

"Half off, huh?" answered Dunhuang, "Why don't we just trade? Take whatever DVD you like."

The guy picked a Chow-Yun Fat movie, *A Better Tomorrow*. Just like a lot of girls, he liked Chow-Yun Fat's smile.

Dunhuang read all the way back to his underground bunk bed. He washed quickly and got into bed, continuing through a criticism of Hong Kong films. This was familiar territory— he'd seen nearly all the movies mentioned in the essay, which made it even more satisfying to read. His roommates didn't straggle in until after ten thirty that night. One of them was applying for a masters degree in Peking University's department of foreign languages—he had a fat, foreigner-loving face. Another was applying for a masters degree in mathematics. He wore glasses and was obviously malnourished, with a pointy chin and a body like a giant question mark. The third was applying for a doctorate in the philosophy department. He had poor eyesight but still looked at you over the top of his glasses, as if they hung on his nose just for decoration.

They didn't have much reaction to their new roommate, only remarking politely, "You're new, eh?"

"I'm new," replied Dunhuang. Then they lined up and took turns in the toilet. The philosophy student was first in and first out. When he looked up and saw Dunhuang was reading an academic work on film, he asked, "Are you in the film department or the Chinese department?"

Dunhuang thought, then said, "Film department." He didn't see much point to studying Chinese. What could you be afterwards but a secretary or something, scribbling down the bullshit your leader spouted, or spouting bullshit yourself? The arts are cooler. Listen to this: "Oh, I'm in the arts."

"Masters program or a doctorate?"

"Doctorate," said Dunhuang modestly. "Just for fun."

The philosophy student's eyes, small and spiritless, immediately flashed at him over his Coke-bottle glasses—Dunhuang thought he looked foolish. "We're in the trenches together then, I'm also applying for a doctorate, in philosophy."

Dunhuang ducked his head, a little nervous. It was all a big lie, for one thing. For another, of all the academic subjects that hinged on the Chinese language, philosophy was the one he respected the most. That instinctual reverence began while he was studying at his miserable vocational school. He had no idea how you did philosophy. It was mystery upon mystery; you couldn't see it or touch it, and as far as he was concerned it was no different from witchcraft or sorcery. The philosophy student let the conversation drop, and climbed clumsily into bed, his neck craning like a goose as he read the book in his hand. He looked effortful, as if he were trying to glimpse some mysteries clearly, to establish a death grip on them. Dunhuang thought again that there was something foolish about him.

The foreign language student and the mathematics student

weren't impressed with his department of fine arts doctorate, and from the time they entered the room to the time they began grinding their teeth and talking in their sleep, they said nothing more to him. Dunhuang worried briefly that they'd already seen through him; he only relaxed later, once he found out that the three of them hardly spoke at all. You could understand a little coolness between competitors, but they were applying to different schools—why the tension? He didn't get it. Dunhuang continued reading, and he thought with chagrin that if he had put in a little more effort early on who could say but he might actually be a Peking University masters or doctoral student—at the very least he could make it into the film academy after watching so many movies.

Early the next morning, his roommates got up and went to the university to eat breakfast and study. Dunhuang was in no hurry—no one was buying DVDs at this time of the morning. He didn't get up until eight, had soy milk and fried dough at a stand at the gate of Chengzeyuan, then decided to sell movies at People's University and then Shuang'an mall. Zhongguancun street was already jammed, like it was every day from morning till night. Why would you build a road just to have it jam up with traffic? Dunhuang thought about that on the bus, as they moved fifty meters in ten minutes. He decided to get off and walk, thinking of a pretentious phrase: a person lived only to die. The university gate was deserted, and Dunhuang worried he'd be too obvious there, so he headed toward Shuang'an. When he reached the other side of the street a few women came up to him, every one of them—how bizarre—carrying an infant. They said:

"Need an ID? Or receipts?"

"Since when do you sell receipts?" asked Dunhuang.

"We've always sold them!" they replied. "What do you need?"

"I used to sell IDs," he said, "but we never sold fake receipts."

The women exchanged glances. One of the infants started crying, and the woman holding him snapped, "What are you bawling about? Little asshole!" The other women glared at Dunhuang and walked off. He was secretly pleased, thinking *Shit, that was actually meant for me!* He really hadn't heard of selling fake receipts before—apparently more and more people were squeezing reimbursements for expenses out of the government these days.

He'd only gone a few steps before another child-laden woman approached him. She was dark and thin, probably from the countryside. The child, sucking its fingers, was strapped to her waist. She came close and said, "You want DVDs? I've got all kinds."

Dunhuang looked at her empty hands. "Where are they?"

She gestured at the building by the side of the road, her finger pointing vaguely toward the back of it. At first, he thought he'd go with her for a look, but then decided there was no point. He pretended he'd just gotten a text message and said someone was looking for him, he had to go. Disappointed, the woman called after him that he should come back any time, she was always there.

He ran into a few more sellers of DVDs and fake IDs. By and large they were women, and the majority of them carried nursing children. The children were there as an insurance policy, of course: *Go ahead and arrest me, are you going to take responsibility for feeding my kid, too?* He also noticed that the police were active in the area, which was why the women did their business empty-handed. Dunhuang thought better of setting up shop—it was too tight. He went to Mudan Gardens, over by Beitaipingzhuang.

Business was lukewarm over the next couple days of roving sales. By the third day, he was in trouble—all his popular movies were sold and choices were limited. What he had left wasn't enough to attract eyeballs. The DVDs had only been meant to last a day. By the afternoon of the third day he had nothing left he could sell, and he packed it in early. He was at a loss. He had no way of restocking, and he regretted not working with Xiaorong. She wouldn't necessarily have been willing, of course—people often wanted to keep their sources secret. Just like when he and Bao Ding were drumming up business—they'd meet their clients at appointed places, and wouldn't tell anyone where. Dunhuang thought a couple times about calling Xiaorong, but each time closed his phone after dialing a few digits. He knew he had no business being jealous, but it bothered him to think that it was the hand of some guy named Kuang Shan, not his own, parked on Xiaorong's thigh. It made his teeth ache to think that she allowed someone else's hand on her thigh. He kept sticking his phone back in his pocket. This was going nowhere. He was just burning himself up. Dunhuang went to a small restaurant and ate three steamed buns before the ache in his teeth faded. Then he strolled very slowly back to Chengzeyuan. On the way, he passed by a shop selling five- and ten-kuai pirated books, and he bought another collection of essays on cinema—he'd finished the first one. When he'd nearly reached the Haidian sports gymnasium, it was Xiaorong who called him.

"Have you sold them all?"

"Yeah," he answered.

"So why didn't you call me?"

"I only just ran out."

On the other end of the line, Xiaorong stayed silent for a full two minutes. Dunhuang stayed silent longer.

"Come and get more," she said finally. "He's not here." She hung up.

By the time Dunhuang got to Furongli she had already arranged the DVDs by type—several of each. They didn't look at one another, staring at the movies as they spoke, as if they were addressing the characters in the films. "That should be enough for three days," she said, turning a DVD over in her hands. "The other kind is still under the bed, if you want them you can take them." He bent down and pulled a stack of porn out from under the bed. Turning his head, he saw Xiaorong's feet in her slippers, her gray socks seemed to warm him. He raised his head, his gaze traveling up her leg, all the way up past her breasts to her face. She immediately looked away. He stood very slowly, then swept her onto the bed. The porn scattered across the floor. She cried out, and only then did Dunhuang feel a little surprised at himself. But it was too late for them to stop. She pushed half-heartedly at him once, then once again, but then she wrapped her arms tighter and tighter around his back.

Things began in haste and eagerness, but then unfolded leisurely, like a silent film from the twenties or thirties. When they finished, it was a drawn-out sigh drifting in on the wind. Afterwards, Dunhuang didn't know what to do. He buried his face in her breasts, silent, then got up and dressed. He gathered the DVDs, shouldered his bag, and got ready to leave. Xiaorong said, "Do you think Beijing's a good place?"

"Pretty good," he answered.

"I still want to go back," she said.

As he understood it, what she meant was: one day she would go back to her hometown, and she would go back with Kuang Shan. But Dunhuang pictured a string of women, women with children at their breast or on their back, each one asking, "are you looking for DVDs? Need an ID?" Dunhuang noticed, for the first time, four fine wrinkles at the corners of Xiaorong's eyes, two on each side. They would soon be joined by others like them.

Before he left he said, "You should go back."

They hadn't discussed what would happen when the DVDs were all sold, and when he needed more the next day, he hesitated before calling her. He told her that a student at Peking University needed thirty-five copies of *Der Himmel über Berlin*. Xiaorong hung up, then called back and said no problem, he could come get them that night.

When Dunhuang arrived they were fighting. Kuang Shan was a tall, skinny man in his early thirties, with a clearly-defined little mustache. The argument interrupted, Kuang Shan grinned and shook his hand, saying Xiaorong had told him Dunhuang was like a younger brother to her. How was he finding the job?

"It's not bad," Dunhuang answered, looking at Xiaorong sitting on the bed, having wept so hard she was hiccupping, her neck stretched forward as she tried to catch her breath. Years ago he'd seen his mother cry this way, when she and his father were getting a divorce. "Xiaorong, sis, is something wrong?"

Kuang Shan waved a hand. "She's just making a scene. Women, right? It's never really that big a deal."

She slumped sideways on the bed, her sobs rising again.

"What are you doing to her?" Dunhuang's face darkened.

"It has nothing to do with you. Take your DVDs and get out." Kuang Shan looked sidelong at Dunhuang. "Leave our cut here." Dunhuang didn't move. "What?" said Kuang Shan. "You don't want the movies?" Xiaorong stopped crying. She came over and pushed Dunhuang, trying to get him to leave. She couldn't budge him. Kuang Shan's face turned ugly—he didn't know about the two of them, but he could tell something wasn't right with Dunhuang. "I can't have a fight with my old lady, huh?" he said.

"Who's your old lady?" exclaimed Xiaorong. "I'm not your anything!"

"Don't push it!" said Kuang Shan. "I'd slap you even if he was your real brother."

Then Dunhuang's fists were flying, and Kuang Shan bled from both nostrils. Xiaorong hadn't expected Dunhuang to act so swiftly, and he was forced back a step as she thrust him bodily toward the door. Kuang Shan's temper flared and he moved to strike back. "You fucking hit me! Where the fuck do you get off hitting me?" Dunhuang's fist flew over Xiaorong's head and landed on Kuang Shan's left eye. "That's right," he said. "And there's more where that came from!"

"Okay!" Kuang Shan sputtered. "So you sicced your beast of a brother on me! Stick around if ya got the balls!"

Dunhuang wanted to laugh—the guy even trotted out Beijing slang when he got angry. *"Ya…?" Do y'think that's all it takes to be a Beijinger, you ass?* Xiaorong shoved him out the door before he could say anything more. She said, "I'm begging you Dunhuang, don't cause trouble for me." Dunhuang's fire died down a little, and he tossed the money through the door before turning and heading down the stairs. Kuang Shan was desperate to retrieve a little face, and came rushing out of the apartment to continue the fight. Xiaorong couldn't stop him, and as Dunhuang emerged from the building he came down the stairs, cursing all the way.

"Stop right there!"

Dunhuang turned to look at him, saying "what the hell d'ya want?" He took a step forward.

Kuang Shan instinctively took a step back. "What gives you the fucking right to hit me?" he asked again.

Dunhuang looked up and saw a head peering out of a third-story window. His voice abruptly softened. "You should treat her better," he said. "A woman like that."

"She treats me like shit, why should I treat her well? And who sent ya to just parachute in and hit me?" Kuang Shan was yelling, waking nearby porch lights with sound-activated switches. Dunhuang could suddenly see the veins and tendons in his neck.

He was preparing to get back into it when Xiaorong called "Dunhuang!" from overhead. And Dunhuang knew he'd been beaten. It suddenly struck him as funny—no one had even arranged a match, and here he was declaring himself the challenger. What right did he have to challenge? He was nothing but an "adopted brother." The "brother" called to the "sister" upstairs: "Don't worry, I'll just take my brother-in-law here for a drink or two and we'll be fine." He turned to Kuang Shan, "Let's go, my treat."

"A drink?" Kuang Shan said, struggling to keep up. "Drink what?"

8

The restaurant, just outside the gate of Furongli, was called The People's Hearth. Dunhuang ordered ten bottles of beer, a few small dishes, and twenty kebabs. He wasn't particularly in the mood to drink that night, it was just a way of handling Kuang Shan—they couldn't have gone on slugging it out with Xiaorong watching. And anyway, there was no great harm in getting drunk.

"Five bottles each," Dunhuang said.

"Five bottles?" Kuang Shan eyed the beer arrayed before him, muddled. He gritted his teeth and said "okay," determined to suffer no further losses.

Dunhuang pushed the beer on him mercilessly. He didn't want to waste too much breath on the guy—the sooner he was good and drunk the sooner the whole thing would be over. Kuang Shan could hold his alcohol, but after the first onslaught he slowed down—not because he was trying to get out of it, but because he couldn't resist the urge to talk. Dunhuang noticed he was starting to slur, and as he slurred his gaze softened, and he took on the look of someone who'd met a childhood friend in an unexpected place. Though the drinks had reddened his face and thickened his neck,

Dunhuang thought he looked a little more sincere like that, at least preferable to the way he preened his little mustache when he was sober.

"Are you really Xiaorong's adopted brother?"

"You doubt it?"

"And that's why you hit me?"

"You were making her unhappy."

"I'm the fucking unhappy one! You think it's easy, running all over the map? Even my dreams are about making money and getting rich, and making a life for myself in this damned place."

"That's your business. She wants to go home."

"My ass! Is there gold and silver waiting at home? We've been here for five years, it's too late to go back. We'd be broke. And things are just getting off the ground for me here, I've got to take care of things. I'm going to let them know that Kuang Shan made something of himself!"

Dunhuang watched Kuang Shan, turning his beer glass and grinning. *You will, will you? Hah.* "Drink!"

Kuang Shan downed his beer. "Brother," he said, leaning his head in and perching a heel on his chair. Dunhuang watched his foot tremble—a guy like this would be better off back at home. "Didn't Xiaorong tell you? I opened a DVD shop, with a friend of course. Business is good—peddlers like you come to me to restock. How can I leave now? Running a shop's hard. This is Beijing, not back home, where you can just set up a shack anywhere you like. You know what I mean?"

"No."

"You and your 'sister' are the same, don't you see? You don't get it. I told her I'll be boss, and she'll be the boss's lady. She won't have to run around with a sack of DVDs, she can just watch the shop while someone else makes deliveries. But she won't do it, she wants to go home. A husband, a kid, and a hot brick bed—it's the peasant mindset! The small-town mindset! You know small-town people? See, you're both the same, you can't accept new things. She thinks that once she's caught up in the store she'll never get out, so she won't even go there unless she's picking up movies. She won't even lend a hand. Listen, Xiaorong's great in every other way but this—she doesn't understand me. She wouldn't even sell DVDs if there was anything else to do. She's drawn a line in the sand!"

"You know why she's in a hurry to go home?"

"I told you—it's just peasant thinking, small-town thinking."

"You're wrong," said Dunhuang, wishing he could dump the whole beer bottle down Kuang Shan's throat. "She's a grown woman, haven't you thought of that? Twenty-eight, on her way to thirty. She'll be old soon. She said to me once, 'how many thirties has a girl got?' She wants a stable home, wants a kid, wants to stop floating, wants a place she can call her own."

"That's what I said! The small-town mindset!" Kuang Shan took a contemptuous swig. "What am I trying to make all this money for if not to give her a home? Someplace that's hers, where she can have a kid?"

The last ten skewers arrived. Fragrant, cumin-smelling lamb.

"You're doing it for yourself," Dunhuang said. "Do you deny it?"

"I swear to heaven and earth…" Kuang Shan trailed off, picking up a skewer. The meat thickened his voice. "Sure, I'm doing it for me, but if you're a man, you've got to do something, that's all. Don't you want to be successful? Don't you want to make something of yourself in this damned place? Sure, I've got my own plans, but you can't say the work and the money don't benefit her." Sulking, he ate three skewers in a row, then, feeling better, continued. "Tell me the truth, brother. If you were me, would you go back home or not?"

"I'm not you."

"But if you were, what would you do?"

"If I was single, of course I wouldn't go back. If I had Xiaorong..." He hesitated. Kuang Shan stared at him while he finished his glass. "I don't know."

Kuang Shan started laughing. "You too, you see? Men are all the fucking same, it's just pots and kettles."

Kuang Shan pissed Dunhuang off, but now they'd somehow become pots and kettles. That nasty little mustache was still bothering him—he wished he could reach over and yank it off. He tamped down his anger. "Drink up."

The mustache was quivering in satisfaction. "I will! I would have anyway!" He was drinking in celebration, Dunhuang was drinking in mourning. He was disappointed in himself. Even if he had Xiaorong, he would just be another fucking Kuang Shan, and not the Dunhuang he was in his imagination.

In the end, Dunhuang only succeeded in getting himself drunk. As soon as he was out the door he vomited violently, a stream of beer, meat, bile, snot, and tears. Kuang Shan asked if he should take him home but Dunhuang shook his head, telling him to go on ahead. Before he left, Kuang Shan told him that if he ever needed DVDs he should come straight to the store to get them.

Dunhuang sat by the Wanquan river until after midnight, then went back to his basement room. The three graduate students were asleep and the room was filled with the sounds of snores and grinding teeth. He washed briefly, and slept until ten thirty the next morning. When he woke the philosophy student was looking through the bag of movies he'd tossed on the table the night before. He had pulled out a porn, and was slavering over the tits and ass on the cover.

"Like it?" asked Dunhuang, sitting up in bed. "You can have it."

The student nearly had a heart attack, and tossed the movie back in the bag as if it had burned him. He laughed awkwardly. "I don't like that stuff," he said, then followed that up with a bitter: "I've got nowhere to watch it, anyway."

It was true, thought Dunhuang, he didn't have a DVD player. The student asked about Dunhuang's bag of DVDs, so he explained, "I know someone who sells movies, this belongs to him. I'm helping him sell a few."

"You mean, you sell pirated DVDs?" The whites of his eyes were showing.

"More or less," Dunhuang answered. He didn't think that idiotic expression augured well for the guy's academic career. He decided to ignore him and hopped off the bed to go wash, his head still big from the night before. He left the apartment, bought a corn-on-the-cob outside the gate of Chengzeyuan, and ate as he walked, heading to Peking University to deliver *Der Himmel über Berlin* to the student named Huang.

You couldn't get into the dorm building without a card, so Huang came downstairs and swiped him in. His roommates wanted to see what other DVDs he had. The dorm was full of graduate students from the Chinese and art departments, and they came to Dunhuang with cash in hand. It was a good day, he thought—everywhere he went, students crowded around his bag. He liked the willingness of real graduate students to spend money. Nearly everyone had their own computer to watch movies on, and they bought stacks of them—porn too. One guy was supposedly writing a novel with some sex scenes in it, but didn't have a girlfriend, so he picked out porn featuring every different race and nationality and bought one of each. For research purposes. In addition to the pre-order of thirty DVDs, Dunhuang sold forty-five more in the space of two hours. It wasn't until someone said an administrator was coming for an inspection that he packed up and left. Huang came down to swipe him out and Dunhuang gave him two popular Hollywood movies for free, arranging to come back the next week.

That kind of bulk sale was pure windfall, though, so Dunhuang kept up his usual rounds.

The basement lodging may have been gritty, but it was cheap, and water and electricity were free. Dunhuang couldn't be bothered to move and decided he'd stay until he'd earned enough money to rent his own place, and buy a TV and DVD player, too. He had a lot of movies to watch. After reading a couple more film books he'd developed an interest in art films. At the end of the week he paid another week's rent, and continued selling DVDs, leaving early and coming back late, exchanging the occasional chat with one of the nerds, enjoying the game of pretending to be an art student. He went as far as to shave his head, one fine morning beside the Wanquan river.

He'd left the basement at mid-morning and taken the path along the river in the park. In a patch of riverside sunlight, four barbers had set up chairs. Practitioners of that ancient craft could set up shop anywhere, all it took was a high-backed wooden chair, basin and basin-stand, cold water in a bucket and hot water in a thermos, manual clippers, a shiny strop, and an old guy in glasses and a white coat, but you didn't even see them in the countryside anymore. Dunhuang had a sudden urge to get his head shaved. When he was young his father had cut his hair for him, with clippers—either a bowl-cut or a flat-top. When he got older, he protested—his father never learned anything but those two dorky styles. He started going to barbershops and hair salons where gentle girls washed his hair. It was no longer a haircut, it was "getting my hair done." Now, standing in the sunlight, he wanted his head shaved. He said to one of the old men, "Need it shaved."

The man craned his neck to look at him, and when he was finally sure he'd heard him correctly, he laughed. It was one of those laughs of deep satisfaction, as though the head were already shaved. Dunhuang threw himself into a chair the likes of which he hadn't touched in years; the three other chairs beside him were all occupied by old men. Old men shaving old men. His barber turned on the radio, first tuning it to Peking Opera, then to a pop station. Dunhuang heard Zhang Huimei's voice straining at the top of her register as she wailed on some mountaintop.

"Flat-top?" the barber asked.

"No top."

"All off?"

"All off."

He closed his eyes while the man worked, and the radio played one pop song after another. The old barber wasn't listening, and hummed a bit of Peking opera to himself, something from *Su San Sent Out Under Guard.* The warm sunlight was like hands caressing his increasingly-exposed scalp, and Dunhuang's thoughts grew turbid and vague, as if he was dreaming, as if he was traveling back to when he was small. Having his father cut his hair in the summer dusk, and afterwards washing in the river, wearing some old long johns of his father's that hung below his knees, and not even underpants underneath. He'd plunge straight in, and when he came up his head would be clean.

His shaved head made his body feel lighter and his feet

fleeter. He sold DVDs in four different places, and it was eleven by the time he returned home. When he walked in the philosophy student asked him, point-blank, "Have you seen my cellphone?" Dunhuang said he hadn't, then put down his bag and went to the toilet. When he came out again he noticed something was wrong. The students of foreign languages and mathematics were rooting under the beds and in the corners like mice, while the philosophy student stared at Dunhuang as if he was drunk, the whites of his eyes growing wide.

"You really haven't seen it?" he asked.

"I really haven't," said Dunhuang, shaking his head just in case he wasn't making himself understood.

"This place must be fucking haunted!" the philosophy student said. He'd put his cellphone on the table before he went to sleep the night before, but had forgotten to take it with him when he left in the morning. When he got back it was gone. "There's only the four of us here, that's eight hands—where would a ninth hand have come from?"

"Unless it was a ghost, it had to have been one of us," said the mathematics student, his expressionless face drawing even longer.

"It must've been," agreed the pudgy language student. "Maybe we should report it?"

Dunhuang looked from one to the other and discovered that all three were looking at him. He took a big step back, then raised a hand and said, "Sure, I vote we report it."

The philosophy student called 110. On the phone he kept repeating the phrase, "you can't judge a book by its cover." Dunhuang thought this was a senseless thing to keep saying. The four of them stayed silent until the police arrived. After a few questions, they were all taken to the police station to make a report. The four were questioned separately, the philosophy student first, then the pudgy language student, then the skinny mathematician, and finally, Dunhuang. It was 1:20 in the morning at that point. He'd spent the whole time up until then sitting in a chair and looking at two girls opposite him. They'd also come to make a report—a theft. They also lived in a collective dormitory. Half of their Chinese was rural dialect, and the two obviously came from different places, but they appeared to have found a common enemy. They were both wearing low-necked little shirts over round white breasts, and as they spoke they threw glances toward Dunhuang instead of looking at each other. So the wait went by quickly, and he wasn't nervous like the last time he'd been caught. As far as he was concerned, he was only here, in the police station in the middle of the night, to look at buxom girls.

"You really didn't see anything?" the officer asked.

"I really didn't," Dunhuang said.

The officer was tired. He lit a cigarette, dragged, and took a long time exhaling. Through the smoke he said, "I hear you're selling pirated DVDs?"

"I don't sell them." Dunhuang got nervous. "I'm just helping a friend temporarily."

"You do know that selling pirated DVDs is illegal?" The officer was making notes.

"I know, of course I know. I'll give him the movies back right away. I'm applying for my doctorate—really, I'm in the doctorate program in Peking University's art department."

"Oh…a doctorate."

"Right, a doctorate. I really didn't see that phone, honestly. I don't even know what it looks like."

"So it was a ghost."

"Sure, it was a ghost." Dunhuang felt a little more relaxed. "Like they said—a ninth hand appeared."

The officer laughed, then pushed his notebook over and said, "Take a look, sign it if everything's in order." After he'd signed, the officer added, "Watch it with the DVDs, there's going to be a crackdown."

The only result of the night's investigation was a pile of documents—the whereabouts of the phone remained unknown. The doctoral student kept persisting until the officer finally said, "That's enough for tonight, there's no need to create bad blood. We'll come visit you in the morning, I can't imagine the thing sprouted wings. None of you are to leave before ten."

They walked back together, in unprecedented unity, along the way discussing what grisly end the phone might have met, then sighing over Beijing's crime, then complaining over the high price of phones, the unfairness of two-way charges, and so on, as if the loss of the phone had no direct connection to them. When they reached the basement room and saw the empty table, however, the shadow of the theft fell over them once more. "My phone…," said the doctor. No one comforted him, they said nothing. They washed up in turns and went to bed.

Dunhuang woke suddenly at around five in the morning, something that had never happened before. The pudgy master's student was snoring and the skinny one occasionally ground his teeth disconsolately—as if he had a rat caged in his mouth. By the light spilling in from the corridor, Dunhuang could see his bag of DVDs on the table, and knew why he'd woken. Gingerly, he got out of bed and dressed, stuffing a few clothes and his toiletries into his bag, and headed for the door. They were still asleep. He closed the door, but then, feeling that vanishing in the night like this was too suspicious, he left a little note on the handle of the door: "If I stole the phone, may I lose a hand to rot and marry a wife with no asshole."

He had paid rent through another two days, but Dunhuang couldn't help that. If he had to lose the forty kuai then so be it. It was better than letting the police confiscate all his DVDs. Without the DVDs he'd have to start all over again.

That day, Dunhuang was the first to arrive at Three Corners, looking on the billboards for information on rooms to rent. By seven thirty he had called the numbers of five different landlords. One didn't answer. Another said his place was rented. Two said they were busy that morning, and he should call back in the afternoon. The fifth was an old lady who hadn't gotten out of bed yet, and spoke thickly. She had a private room, in Weixiuyuan, four hundred a month—four hundred and fifty with utilities added. It was just about the cheapest of all the rooms advertised at Three Corners. Dunhuang was interested.

The landlady wasn't as old as he'd imagined; she wasn't yet sixty and was dressed fairly well. She said she'd been Party secretary in some government-owned business before she retired. Dunhuang thought she looked the part, but who knew—there were no rules about what a Party secretary should look like. Her bad breath was disappointing, though. Even more disappointing was the room itself—he hadn't realized that the so-called private room was the shack behind him, barely taller than he was. It had been hastily erected in the middle of the courtyard, the walls a single layer of brick, the ceiling a few concrete slabs, and above that a sloping roof of asbestos tile to keep the rain from running inside. It would truly take a miracle of architecture to turn a shack like this into an apartment. Inside was a bed, a table, a stool, a little bookshelf, and nothing else—nor was there room for anything else.

"Can you go a little lower?"

"Not a penny. It's a private room, very quiet. I'm only renting it to you because you're a Peking University student... You're not? Well, a prospective student is fine too, you'll get there eventually."

Private room. Private room. Dunhuang poked around the room, accidentally pulling the light cord and bathing the white-washed walls in brilliance. He suddenly realized how good it would be to have his own place. He could buy a television and watch his movies; he would have somewhere to retreat to during Beijing's nights, where the wind couldn't reach him, nor the rain wet him. He was unable to stand the landlady's breath any longer, so he said, "All right. One condition: I pay rent monthly. I'm still waiting on some cash from home."

"Well, okay." The landlady pinched her chin thoughtfully, a very Party secretary gesture. "I'll need a month's deposit, though. This month's rent now, and next month's in advance."

Dunhuang knew what "deposit" meant. She was afraid her renter would skip out, possibly cleaning out her valuables in the process. *There's just these two pieces of broken furniture*, thought Dunhuang, *they're no treasure. You couldn't even give them away.* He rented the room, though, paying two months' rent—nearly everything he had. After cleaning up a bit he sat on the edge of the bed and discovered he was starving. He'd get some food, then go sell DVDs. He needed money.

9

With lodgings taken care of he felt like he'd finally put down roots. Now he could proceed with a more orderly plan for the future. He would spend his days selling DVDs to make money, of course, but he would also find some time to visit Bao Ding. Ideally, he'd locate Qibao before that—he didn't want to disappoint Bao Ding.

The problem was where to look. Besides her name and the fact that she sold fake IDs, plus that one glimpse of her back, he knew nothing about her, not even her surname. As long as she was still in Beijing selling fake IDs he stood a chance, otherwise he wouldn't even know which haystack to go needle-hunting in. If only Bao Ding had seen fit to mention her earlier, instead of waiting until the police were hauling them off. It was his fault too—he'd thought that, as long as he had his freedom, finding someone would be a piece of cake, and he hadn't asked for more details. His preliminary plan was to sell DVDs and look for her at the same time—his chances of finding her rose with the number of places he visited. He'd get to know the fake ID crowd, make some inquiries. He'd keep an eye out as he sold movies, and look over the girls, specifically their backs and asses. He thought he would be able to pick her ass out of a crowd.

He looked at countless asses over the next few days—big and small, fat and skinny, round and flat, overripe and undeveloped, shapely and shapeless—until he began to see cheeks even with his eyes closed. The majority of asses are unappetizing. Dunhuang realized that the plan was impractical, he simply couldn't keep them all straight. The unpleasant ones were each unpleasant in their own way, but the nice-looking ones were more or less similar. It would never work. He asked various fake ID peddlers in various places if they'd heard of a girl named Qibao. A third shook their heads. A third responded by asking him if he wanted a fake ID—they could get him anything. The last third just glared or swore at him. Dunhuang had to admit it was laughable to go around asking everyone he met, as if he were a character in some fairy tale.

It didn't hurt to ask, however, and not asking was guaranteed to get him nowhere, so he kept it up. But he'd mostly given up any hope of getting results. There were so goddamned many fake ID sellers in Beijing, enough to make up a little town of their own. To keep the search interesting, he thought of it as a special way of interacting with strangers, beyond selling them DVDs. Sometimes, after the movies were sold, he'd ask his customers randomly, "Do you know a girl named Qibao?"

The customers looked at him quizzically, and hurried off. He'd smile apologetically at their backs.

As long as the weather held, he could make money every day. He saved what he could, calculating how many days it would be before he could buy a television and a DVD player. When he needed more DVDs he didn't call Xiaorong, he went straight to the store called Cosmic that Kuang Shan ran with his friend—he didn't want to disturb Xiaorong at home. But they continued their relationship quietly. Put gently, they lent each other warmth. Put less gently, it was adulterous.

Dunhuang couldn't care less about adultery—as a single man the worst he'd get was a beating. But he worried about Xiaorong. He could tell she was the sort to take things to heart, but when they met they couldn't help themselves. Afterwards, he'd pull on his pants and take off, but how much longer could she be caught between two men? It had to end—they should end it. He thought she probably felt the same way. One day she called him, at first accusing him bitterly of not coming to see her, but soon softening. Dunhuang said he'd just gone to Kuang Shan's place to pick up movies, then added that he would come see her whenever she was next free. She fell silent, and they ended the conversation without her ever telling him when she would be free. So Dunhuang made the sad decision. A short, sharp pain was better than dragging things out, and as the man he should be the one to end it.

Then it was done, and after that they met only rarely, and hardly even talked on the phone again.

Cosmic was in an alley off Saoziying, and its walls were plastered with garish movie posters. To the left of the door was the shop name, and on the right a sign: guaranteed legal! The shelves in the shop held mostly authorized copies, but that was just for show. The pirated stuff was through a side door, and that's where most of the business went on. The first time Dunhuang went to the store, Kuang Shan introduced him to Boss Zhou, his partner, and to the two shop assistants, introducing him as Xiaorong's adopted brother. *He's a buddy of mine, give him a discount.* The shop assistants, a girl and a boy, both in their early twenties, seemed to know a lot about movies. Hand them a DVD and they could tell you all about it: the story, the director, the actors, its critical reception, its meaning—they even knew the secret behind-the-scenes gossip. Dunhuang said he was in awe. They said, "It's no big deal. We just watch a lot of movies."

Thirteen days after moving into Weixiuyuan, Dunhuang bought a television and a DVD player. The DVD player was new; the TV came from a second-hand market, lightly-used, two hundred kuai. It looked good. He ate two packets of instant noodles that night, and watched four movies in a row. Well after midnight he went out to use the bathroom. A strong night wind was blowing over the asbestos tiles, and grit got in his eyes. Instead of going to the public toilet at the mouth of the alley, he just pissed beneath the scholar tree at the entrance to the yard and hurried back. *Fucking sandstorms, showing up in the middle of the night.*

The next morning he heard someone talking excitedly outside his window about the dust. He couldn't get back to sleep, so he got up and went outside to find them still talking. His landlady pointed at his feet and said Look, young man, dust. Dunhuang looked down to see a thick layer of fine yellow dust under his feet. He stomped one foot and raised a little cloud, then stomped again and raised another. He stomped a dozen times and dust rose into the air; his landlady and neighbor backed away yelling, "Stop it! Stop it! We're choking!"

He stopped. "Where'd this come from?" Everything around him was covered with a thick layer of yellow. "The sandstorm?" The wind had stopped and the sun was in the sky, though it looked white from all the sand still in the air. Yellow sky, white sun.

"It rained dust!" his landlady said excitedly. "The heavens rained dust on us!"

All the neighbors were excited, old and young. All these years—who had ever seen it rain dust? Dunhuang had never seen it, anyway. He gave the scholar tree a kick, and yellow dust came floating down. It had actually rained fucking dust. Dunhuang got excited too. He washed, packed his bag, and got to work. Everything he saw was covered in dust, glistening yellow or dingy gray. Plenty of kids were stomping, too. In some places the street-sweepers were still sweeping, and the dust was piled high at the sides of the streets. Bizarre. No wonder he and his friends had all ended up in prison—it was a year of bad omens.

What was really fun was being on the pedestrian bridge. From that vantage point he could see how the streets and the low residential buildings had all turned the same dirt-yellow color overnight, the way winter snows might blanket the earth. But the feeling was completely different; it made the dust-covered buildings and streets look like ancient ruins, silent and deathly. It was hard to believe there was something besides snow that could make the whole world appear so simple and two-dimensional, and at the same time so decayed and desolate. Watching the expressionless faces of the people hurrying by, Dunhuang was overcome by a sudden hopeless lust, and he shouted, "Xia—Xiao—Rong!"

No one knew who Xiaorong was, but they all turned their heads to look at the curious madman. He nodded and smiled at them with private pleasure, the way they abruptly turned their heads and bodies in concert seemed to swing the whole world into motion. He noticed a car parked by the side of the road, in the dust covering it, someone had written:

Fucking sandstorm

This seemed like fun to Dunhuang, so he trotted down from the bridge and added: *But of course.* He observed his handiwork with pleasure, feeling a bit of his old calligraphic skills returning. When he was in middle school there was a bit of a calligraphy fad, and anyone who could hold a pen was practicing. He went along with the fad, first using a broken branch to practice in the sandy riverbank outside the school gates—he'd write, let the waves wash it away, then write again. Later, he used a brush and water, writing on the concrete in the sunlight. By the time he got to the end of what he was writing, the beginning had begun to dry, and he would trace over the disappearing characters. There were crowds of kids out there on the sidewalk at noon, their rear ends all raised high—quite a sight. Writing "But of course" wasn't enough, though, so he went around to the trunk of the car and wrote: *I didn't write this.*

Then he went on his way. He noticed a BMW parked on the street, so he went up to it and wrote: *Fucking BMW*

He did it on three more cars in a row, changing the brand for each one. He reached the fifth car and was about to write "fucking," when he remembered how they'd once left ads for fake IDs, in permanent ink or spray paint, in places where pedestrians might notice: *Fake IDs, call 130...* Why not leave an ad for DVDs? So he wrote his own number: *DVDs, call 133...*

He was pleased with this small stroke of genius. He kept it up, writing on every car he passed, on the hood if no one had wiped it off, on the trunk if they had. One after another, until his finger was tingling, his arm sore, and his right hand looked like it was made out of mud. He ignored the people watching him, he concentrated on his writing, and when he was done he moved on. At two in the afternoon he stopped and made a rough tally—at least three hundred cars. He found a hole-in-the-wall restaurant and ordered two beers and a couple of dishes to reward himself. As he drank, he thought with satisfaction, *Now I'll just wait for the orders to come in.* He imagined that, years from now, other DVD sellers would remember him with gratitude as the originator of the DVD delivery service.

Before he finished his meal his phone rang, and he picked up enthusiastically. The caller said, "Are you the guy selling DVDs?"

"That's right. What would you like to see, miss?"

"Are you a fucking idiot?"

That wasn't what he'd intended. Dunhuang tried to lighten the tone: "I'm sorry, miss, I don't think I've got that one."

"Don't play cute with me. Listen, don't go scrawling on everything you see, if your little claws itch you can scratch them on a rock!" Then she hung up.

Dunhuang was energized. He took another swallow of beer, and said to himself, *I'll scratch them on your mom's leg!*

Fake ID sellers dealt with this sort of thing all the time. They'd leave an advertisement right where it would piss someone off, or glue a flier to something important, and then get a phone call from some idiot with a temper. Dunhuang was thrilled because his advertisements were having an effect. If one person was willing to spit on him, another might do business.

As he was settling the bill his phone rang again. It was a young man, asking if he had DVDs to sell—he'd seen the ad on a car. Dunhuang said, "That's right, what do you want?" The man said his office was at Changhong Bridge, and he had some co-workers who wanted to browse. Once he got the address, Dunhuang got on a bus. It was four thirty when he arrived. The man, named Yu, was on the fifth floor, and Dunhuang told him he had a big bag of movies he could look through. Several colleagues crowded around, all of them knowledgeable about film. Their offhand comments were all right on the mark, and Dunhuang noticed it was an arts management company. The whole building was arts related—fiction, poetry, theater, and also dance, music, film, and nonfiction publishing. The man named Yu said a DVD seller used to come regularly, but they hadn't seen him in three months. Dunhuang said he'd come regularly from then on, and if they wanted something in particular they could call ahead. The workers were impressed with the quality of his merchandise—something Dunhuang was fairly confident about. They were pirated, but they were pirated well. Honor among thieves, right? He sold thirty-one DVDs.

As he was leaving, Dunhuang asked tentatively: "Can I try these other companies?"

"Sure," said Yu, "just knock on some doors. That's how the last guy did it."

Dunhuang nearly fainted from happiness. Heaven had dropped a penny straight into his pocket. He wandered the building, which was more than ten stories tall, but only got through two floors before the end of the work day. On those two floors alone he sold more than eighty DVDs. More than eighty...it was unreal. Two or three hundred in pure profit. On his way out he grinned so hard at the door guard that the man looked at him uneasily.

"What are you grinning at?"

"Just saying hello," Dunhuang said. "I'll be back tomorrow. They told me to come."

Dunhuang bought a newspaper before he got on the bus, and got a shock. The paper said that the night before more than 300,000 tons of dust had fallen on Beijing. His only handle on the idea of 300,000 tons of dust was to imagine how many grave mounds you could make with it. The paper went on to say that a part of these 300,000 tons was produced in Beijing itself—the city was one huge construction site, and even without the winds the dust still flew. The other part had blown in from the deserts of Xinjiang and Inner Mongolia. Wind was pretty goddamned amazing, carrying all those grains of dust from thousands of kilometers away. Quite a project. There was another bit of startling news—a train in Xinjiang was caught in the sandstorm, and the windows on one side of the train were all broken. The passengers had stuffed the windows with blankets and mattresses to fend off the sand that had come to do battle with them. Dunhuang guessed it wouldn't have been much fun to be there, but he loved reading about it, and wanted to tell someone. But who? There seemed to be no one but the elusive Qibao. *Qibao, Qibao...where are you?*

10

Another trip to Changhong Bridge, another stack of DVDs. He'd have to go restock that afternoon. Kuang Shan was shocked at how often he was coming back to Cosmic, and how well he was doing selling on his own. Dunhuang said, "I've just got one rule: it's life or death. Or if you want to be pretentious about it: professionalism."

And Dunhuang was a professional. Every time he restocked from the shop, he tried the DVDs in his own player to make sure he wasn't selling his customers duds. He'd test at least one movie from each batch. When restocking he picked the highest-quality movies from among the pirated offerings. It didn't matter that they were more expensive—at worst he'd earn a little less—his reputation was paramount. It was another lesson from selling fake IDs: repeat customers were essential. If they were satisfied, they'd do your advertising for you. Timely delivery was also key. And his game with the cars had given him a taste for advertising—he bought a few boxes of self-adhesive labels, wrote his ads on them, and then stuck them in places where people lingered: apartment gates, elevators, lobby entrances. The increased coverage had a noticeable effect: he'd often get calls with orders. Calls from individuals were small sales, sometimes just one or two films, but Dunhuang still did his best to deliver. When he arrived at the meeting place, he'd run his mouth and do his best to sell a few extra. One girl in particular, though, seemed immune to his patter: she only bought one or two movies, never more, and they were always gory horror films.

She lived in Zhichunli, Dunhuang had to pass through most of Zhongguancun to get there. The worst part was there were no good bus routes between Weixiuyuan and Zhichunli, so he had to transfer or walk half the distance. It took him almost an hour to get there the first time. She lived in the innermost building in her compound, on the top floor. She was pretty, but her expression was always cold, like someone owed her money, and she smoked those thin lady's cigarettes, sometimes with a lazy, decadent flair, sometimes with it clamped in her jaw. Her aggravation and anxiety were evident. She wouldn't let him inside, they conducted their transactions through the bars of the security door. Through the door he could see a surprisingly luxurious room, luxurious enough to be shocking. He'd only seen scenes like that on the TV and in movies. He couldn't understand why someone living in heaven on earth would be so bitter and angry. Once, while making a delivery, Dunhuang couldn't help asking, "Why do you always watch violent or scary movies? I've got a lot of art films here, and some romances, classics, award winners…"

Before he could finish, her temper flared. "Just shut up, will you? Do you want me to buy a movie or not?" She hurled her newly-lit cigarette onto the carpet, which began to give off a strange smell.

"I'm sorry, I didn't mean anything by it," Dunhuang said, turning to leave. "Your carpet's on fire."

"I know!" she shouted.

Dunhuang grumbled as he went downstairs. *Who do you think you are? Being pretty doesn't give you the right to have a shitty temper.* He decided he wouldn't deliver to her anymore— it was just a DVD or two, his earnings went straight to the bus conductor, and now he had to get his ear chewed off? But the next time she called to place an order, he went. She was just a girl, why hold a grudge? Also, he continued to be faintly curious about her situation—even a little worried. He'd never seen another person in her room. No matter what else, there was something a little strange about that. Maybe a change of film diet would do her some good. When he was handing over her order Dunhuang thought better of recommending films directly, instead he framed it as small talk, "This apartment complex reminds me of one I saw in a movie. It was a real tear-jerker…I think a girl would need a whole towel to get through it." Or else, "Sorry I'm late, traffic was backed up by an accident. A taxi rammed a police car, pretty stupid, right? That happened in this one movie, too, have you seen it? It's practically as moving as the Bible." He'd read that last line in a book.

At first, the girl's expression was as sardonic as always, like she was watching a circus. She saw right through Dunhuang's little tricks. But after a while her attitude softened and she was a little less impatient. Her cigarette-smoking became a little more graceful as well. But she still never took the bait and asked about other movies. Dunhuang was pleased with this meager success, however, and decided to keep it up. One day, he was sure, the girl would take something other than a violent or scary film.

She called him nearly every other day—Dunhuang considered buying a bicycle. He needed one for the rest of his work, anyway. One morning, he stuck a few want ads for a bike up at Three Corners, and at noon someone called him, asking for a meeting. As it happened, he was selling DVDs not far from Peking University, so he packed his bag and went.

The man was in his early thirties, in a suit and tie, very urbane. He took Dunhuang for a walk past the library, dormitories, and classroom buildings, looking over the rows of bicycles, and asked him what kind of bike he preferred. Dunhuang thought a lightly-used mountain bike would be about right, but was worried he couldn't afford it. The suit said, no problem, we can discuss price. Something like this one here, then?

"Yeah," Dunhuang said. "Or not quite so nice."

"All right then," the suit said. "I'll see you this afternoon outside the west gate."

At five thirty that afternoon, Dunhuang arrived at the west gate to find the man waiting by one of the stone lions, wearing sunglasses and sitting on a bicycle that seemed more familiar the more Dunhuang looked at it. The suit hopped off the bike and pushed it across the street to Weixiuyuan. "The money?" he said.

"It looks exactly like the bike we looked at earlier," Dunhuang said.

"'Looks like'?" the man said with a chuckle. "It is. It's just got a new lock, that's all."

Indeed, the lock was the only difference. At noon it had had two good-quality locks on it; now it just had a cheap wheel-lock. "This is no good," said Dunhuang. "What if someone recognizes it?"

"Fuck, the country's full of bikes exactly like this one," said the suit. "Who's going to recognize it? You're worried? Okay then." He took a little knife out of his pocket and started scratching at the bike, until there were paint chips all over the ground. "Better?"

Dunhuang hesitated. The suit said, "What the fuck is with

you? It's just a bike, I'd hate to watch you trying to find a wife. You'd end up getting dumped, anyway. If you don't want it I'm junking it. That guy thought it would be safe with two locks on it…"

"I do want it," said Dunhuang. "I'm just worried what will happen."

"Fuck-all will happen! How's this, I'll give it to you for eighty, that's twenty off. I'm a good guy, right?"

"All right, deal." Dunhuang got on the bike, and it felt pretty damn good. He was a fucking bicycle owner. When the suit left he told Dunhuang to get another lock, a good one—this kind of bike was always getting stolen. He also gave him a business card, saying if any of his friends needed bikes, one call was all it took. The card read:

Mr. Zhang, General Manager, "Secondhand" Bicycle Store Phone Number: 133…

Dunhuang thought the card was a collector's item. The world was crazy, and this was the proof. He liked his second-hand mountain bike, just being on it made life taste sweeter. Dunhuang had ridden many bikes—Forevers, Phoenixes, Flying Pigeons, even the Shandong-made Great Golden Deer brand—but he'd never ridden one of these, a Giant. A fucking *Giant* mountain bike. He rode the bike to Zhichunli to deliver DVDs to the girl, feeling even more strongly that he ought to rescue her from her world of gore and horror. He even thought she should try some porn, at least she could learn something. What was the point of all the blood and the guts and the midnight rings?

The girl didn't take his advice, but nevertheless something had changed. When she opened the door she wasn't wearing some old pajamas like usual, she had dressed up a little bit, and her hair showed traces of a comb. "Have you ever ridden a Giant bicycle?" Dunhuang asked her. "They're really fucking good. Don't laugh, I just bought one today. All the way here I was thinking life is good. Try it if you don't believe me, I'll lend it to you. It's secondhand, I hope that doesn't bother you."

At last, the "I hope that doesn't bother you" got her to laugh. To be precise, it was half a laugh. When she discovered she was laughing, she cut the second half short.

"Thanks," she said. "Goodbye." She started closing the door.

Dunhuang called through the rapidly-closing crack, "Have you see *The Bicycle Thief*? It's really good!"

When he came out of the building, the bike was gone. He clearly remembered leaving it there, stuck between two other bikes. The other bikes, both of them wrecks, were still there. He searched all around the building, but there was no sign of it. It had been stolen, that was it. Dunhuang thought immediately of the suit. He hunted up the number and called.

"Hello, do you have a friend who wants a bike too?"

"They all drive sedans," said Dunhuang. "My bike's been stolen!"

"You mean, you'd like to buy another?"

"Fuck you, my bike's gone!"

"Call the police, then—what am I going to do about it?"

"Only you knew that bike!"

"Fuck you, shit for brains! If I only dealt in bikes I knew, I'd be out on the street!"

"So how was my bike stolen?"

"Ask the thief! Ask your lock!" The suit was getting mad, too. "You think they come with a lifetime guarantee, you asshole?"

Dunhuang said nothing. He'd forgotten to get a good lock for his Giant. He assumed the bike would be with him during the day, and locked up in his courtyard at night, so he hadn't bothered yet.

"Who told you to pinch your pennies?" said the suit. "Never mind a thief, even a child could break off one of those wheel-locks. Serves you right! I have no sympathy at all! How about I get you another bike? How's fifty percent off?"

"Fuck you!" said Dunhuang, and hung up the phone, heartbroken. The more he thought the madder he got, until he decided to hell with bicycles, people got around fine before bicycles were invented. *I'll run—let's see them steal my legs.*

The next time, he really did run to Zhichunli. He discovered it wasn't actually much slower than the bike. He passed the south gate of Peking University, turned right at Pacific Computer City, crossed Zhongguancun Street and then the Zhongguancun Bridge, carried straight on past the north Fourth Ring Road, turned right onto Science Academy South, and went straight into Zhichunli. As he ran, his spirits rose—he ran right through three red lights, caused two cars to screech to a halt, and was stared at by many. It was rare to see a madman sprinting through bustling Zhongguancun. Once at Zhichunli, Dunhuang slowed his breath before pressing the doorbell. He passed *Kill Bill* and *Banlieue 13* between the bars of the safety door.

The girl was wearing a skirt, and a flame-red shawl. "Thanks," she said. "Have you got that bicycle one you mentioned last time?"

"*The Bicycle Thief?*"

She glanced down for a moment, then said, "That's the one. *The Bicycle Thief.*"

"I've got no bicycle thief, I'm only the bicycle-thieved."

"Is that good, too?"

"I'm joking. I was talking about myself. I've got the movie

at home, I'll bring it next time."

"Your bike was stolen?"

"Yeah, outside your building, when I was here a couple days ago."

"The Giant?"

"The Giant mountain bike."

"How much was it? I'll reimburse you for it."

"Eighty."

"Eighty? A Giant?" The girl finally really laughed, then picked up her wallet from a nearby table and pulled out five hundreds to give to him. "Liar! Giants aren't that cheap. Whatever it really costs, I'm only giving you this, if it's not enough that's your problem."

Dunhuang waved her off. "It really was eighty. Second-hand. Take your money back, it wasn't you who stole it."

The girl stuck her hand out through the door and flapped the cash. "You lost it because of me, of course I should pay. Take it."

"It's not your fault," Dunhuang said. "I'm going, I'll bring you that movie next time." He went downstairs with the girl calling after him.

From then on, as long as the delivery was within three kilometers, Dunhuang did it running. When he was still in school he was a good long-distance runner. He hadn't done it for years and was a little unused to it at first, but soon the feeling came back to him, and he got pleasure from the exercise. The next time he delivered DVDs to the girl, adding *The Bicycle Thief* into the bargain, he ran there again. She still wanted to give him money, or a new Giant if he wouldn't take the money. Dunhuang said, "Absolutely not, I'm loving running, don't burst my bubble. If I don't exercise these 70 kilos will turn to flab."

The girl's eyes grew wide, and she said, "Whoa, you ran here?"

"Yeah. If the lights are green I can run nonstop."

"Look at you bragging!" She looked better laughing than stone-faced, her teeth like jade. "If this movie's no good you're going to hear about it from me!"

11

On the way back from Zhichunli, as he was passing the gate of the Foreign Languages Institute, Dunhuang got an unfamiliar phone call. A man said in a low voice, "I saw your advertisement, are you selling DVDs? I want something hard."

Dunhuang hesitated before saying, "I've got that, how many do you want?"

"The more the better. The north gate of the Beijing University of Aeronautics and Astronautics, I'm wearing a gray jacket and a red tie."

Dunhuang took the bus there. He saw the gray jacket sitting on the curb across from the university, his red tie was very flashy. Dunhuang approached with his bag on his back. "Want a movie?" The jacket nodded.

"Let's find someplace quiet to talk." They turned into an empty street and stopped. Dunhuang pulled three porn DVDs out of the side pocket of his bag.

"Got any more?"

Dunhuang put the bag down at his feet and pulled out another ten. "That's all."

The jacket looked into the open bag. "You've got softcore too?"

Dunhuang pulled five DVDs from the pile, his hand unerring. He didn't have many, softcore didn't sell well. As the jacket flipped through the packages one of his legs shook continuously. Once he'd looked through them all closely, he suddenly yelled, "I'm a police officer!"

Dunhuang blinked, then laughed. "Come on, brother, don't scare me, I have a weak bladder."

"Don't believe me?" The guy stuck his right hand into his pocket and pulled out his ID, flipping it open. He really was police. At the same time, his other hand was already closing on one of the straps of the bag. "I'm confiscating your DVDs!"

Dunhuang pointed at the ground and said, "Is that your money?" When the jacket looked down Dunhuang yanked the bag out of his hand and took off. The jacket tried to grab the bag with his other hand, but it was too late. The strap he was holding tore off, and he let go. He shouted, "Stop!" Dunhuang ran for all he was worth, the bag over one shoulder, DVDs flying from its open mouth. Luckily, he was a fast runner—the jacket gave up after fifty meters. Dunhuang didn't stop until he'd reached the gate of the Science Academy, hastily zipping up the bag as he ran. He checked that the jacket was nowhere in sight before flopping down on the side of the street. His calves were trembling, cramped from fright. He was remembering Haidian Bridge.

But this time he'd gotten away.

It took him the rest of the day to get back to normal—what a fucking awful start to the morning. His heart wasn't in selling DVDs; he was constantly looking around, afraid the police would leap out. He'd lost fewer than 30 DVDs while running, but it was still enough to hurt. In the aftermath, he was not only hyper-vigilant about the police, he also jumped out of his skin every time the phone rang—first was Kuang Shan, using someone else's phone. He was calling just to say that the Korean movie he'd wanted, *The Isle*, had arrived and he could come and pick it up. Dunhuang had already worked himself into a state over whether to pick up the unfamiliar number. The second call was also an unknown number. Dunhuang gritted his teeth and picked up.

The caller said, with no preamble, "Is that you, Crow? You been hiding in Li Xiaohong's underpants again? I haven't seen you for six months!"

Dunhuang let out a breath. "Sorry, you've got the wrong number."

"Like hell I've got the wrong number. I'd know your caw if it came out my ass. Don't ya play with me!"

"I'll repeat myself: y'got the wrong goddamn number!"

"Huh? It's really not you?"

"It's your mom!" Dunhuang hung up. Whoever it was called again, and let it ring until Dunhuang finally picked up again.

The caller hadn't even lost his temper. "I'm sorry I bothered you. Do you know Crow's number? A friend gave me yours."

"Sorry, try the Forbidden City if you're looking for crows. I only know magpies."

Dunhuang felt a little better after that, and he decided to concentrate on selling movies, it was almost evening. He cursed gray jacket as he went, *bullshit cop, bullshit cop…* But a light bulb went on as he approached Haidian—there had been something wrong with jacket's ID. He craned his neck, trying to latch on to the problem. The leather case…the printing… the font…There it was: the last character of the title on the ID had been squeezed up against the margin. There was no way a normal ID would have been that poorly designed. The title had been squeezed on purpose. Bao Ding once got a job like that, and Dunhuang went with him to pick up the finished product. Bao Ding asked if something was wrong with the signature on the ID. The forger said they always did it that way for fake police IDs—they included an imperfection, leaving an out for themselves. It was like counterfeit bills, they always left something wrong in the details. Dunhuang remembered the guy saying, righteously, "It's part of our moral code."

Dunhuang thought carefully about the jacket's ID. There had definitely been something wrong with it. His mood improved immediately, he'd been taken in by a fake! He swore loud enough to shake the sky, and continued on feeling practically carefree, even forgetting his annoyance at the guy looking for Crow. Who could say if it was a wrong number, maybe it was just a bored crank caller? At that point, another light bulb went on—why not use the same trick in his own search for Qibao? Why hadn't he thought of it earlier? Dunhuang was impressed with his own genius—the search was as good as done. What can you do? Sometimes you just get clever.

He turned on the spot and went back the way he'd come, looking for fake ID ads on the sidewalk, bus-stops, traffic control boxes, and trash cans. They read: *IDs, internet connections, receipts,* and each had a phone number. Dunhuang tore off each one he saw, and when he got home he started calling every one of the twenty-two numbers he'd collected.

If a woman picked up, he'd say, "Is this Qibao? I'm Crow."

She'd answer, "No, you've got the wrong number."

He'd continue, "Are you sure? A friend gave me this number. Do you know Qibao?"

"No, I've never heard of her."

"Oh, sorry to bother you then. Thanks."

If a man picked up, he'd say, "Hey, this is Crow. Have you seen Qibao lately?"

The man would say, "Who's Crow? I don't know you. Haven't heard of Qibao either."

"Sorry, wrong number! Thanks."

Southern accents, northern dialects, half-cooked Beijing slang. Those with good tempers would grumble a bit before hanging up. If he got a mean one, though, he was in for a tongue lashing: asshole, bastard, idiot, go to hell, etc.

Then he'd start over with a new number.

He worked through all twenty-two numbers with no success. He wasn't disappointed, though, this was still the best way to find Qibao. He would let the mountain come to Mohammad —he'd be the still point at the center. All he had to worry about was finding advertisements, and that was no problem: while he distributed his own, he could collect others'.

Dunhuang spent a week picking up ads, selling DVDs all the while. When he got home, he'd make calls—no less than three hundred in seven days. He didn't expect Qibao herself to be among the three hundred, but if one of them had even heard of her, he'd be all set. He couldn't expect to cover the entirety of Beijing's fake-ID industry with three hundred numbers, but perhaps it would do for a half, or a third. It was only a matter of time before he found Qibao. He had to keep track of numbers he'd called twice, of course. There were ten or so of those—he'd forgotten which ones he'd already called. After getting a few earfuls, Dunhuang learned his lesson and made a rough list of numbers, checking them off as he went.

Three hundred numbers, but Qibao continued to elude him. Dunhuang surveyed his drawerful of used phone cards, gritted his teeth, and continued dialing. He thought of it as buying Bao Ding a drink. One afternoon, while Dunhuang was selling DVDs by Hangtian Bridge, he saw a boy of roughly ten walking on top of the bridge, bobbing down every few steps.

He was pasting advertisements on the ground. Dunhuang followed him onto the bridge, and saw they were new numbers. He peeled one off the ground and called. It was a woman's voice that answered.

"Is that Qibao? It's Crow!"

"Crow? Haven't heard of you."

"Do you know Qibao?"

"Who are you, really?"

"Do you know Qibao, really?"

"I do."

"Great! I'm Dunhuang, can you tell me where she is?"

"Who the fuck are you, *really*?"

"Dunhuang. I'm Dunhuang. Bao Ding asked me to find Qibao."

"Oh, why didn't you say so? That's me."

"Where are you?"

"In bed."

She lived nearby, in Huayuancun, and had just woken up. Dunhuang suggested they have dinner together, and Qibao said, "Great, I wasn't in the mood to cook." They arranged to meet by a pedestrian overpass near Huayuancun, and Dunhuang sat on the bottom step of the bridge, smoking and rubbing his hands in excitement. Finally, goddamn it, he'd found her. He could stop feeling quite so guilty about Bao Ding. Someone tapped him on the shoulder. He turned around to see a fairly tall, full-figured girl, quite young and pretty. She had long hair in curls, and wore a cardigan, an impractical shawl, and a skirt. The cardigan was open low in front, revealing deep cleavage. Dunhuang wasn't sure if he should think of her as a woman or a girl.

"Qibao?"

"Dunhuang?"

Dunhuang grinned, then stood and circled behind her: there they were, that back and ass he'd been looking for. "What are you doing?" she asked.

Dunhuang quickly replied, "I'll treat you to dinner. Bao Ding gave specific instructions to take care of you."

"So where is he? I never heard from him. He promised to take me to the Great Wall and the Ming Tombs."

"Don't you know? He's in jail. I just got out myself."

"Fuck...I should have guessed. He's really an okay guy." Qibao rummaged around in her pockets and finally said, "Do you have a cigarette?"

Dunhuang passed her one and lit it. "You smoke, huh?"

"I'd die of boredom otherwise," she said. "Today was extra dull, no business. I fell asleep in front of the TV."

They headed toward a Sichuanese restaurant.

"No business, but you hired a kid to paste ads?"

"You saw him, did you? Can't do it myself, can I? I'd be a laughingstock. What treasures have you got in that bag?"

"DVDs. I sell them."

They reached the restaurant. The place was tiny, but when Dunhuang flipped open the menu the prices nearly made him choke. Eighteen kuai for Kungpao chicken—it was shameless. Dunhuang pushed the menu toward Qibao, steeled himself, and said, "You order."

Qibao said, "This place is good, I suggest it anytime a friend offers to treat." She ordered oil-poached fish, buckwheat noodles with chicken slivers, Dongpo pork leg, crockpot greens, and Sichuanese pickled vegetables. *It'll be no worse than being tricked twice by fake policemen*, thought Dunhuang.

"How'd you end up selling pirated DVDs?" asked Qibao. "No more fake IDs?"

"After I got out I couldn't connect with anyone, so I started selling DVDs in the meantime. Now I think it's pretty good work, and I don't want to go back."

"You got to like it, huh?"

"More or less. You don't earn much, but there's less to worry about, and you can watch films in your spare time. Life is pretty good."

"You must have gotten culture in jail," said Qibao. "Did the two of you go in together?"

"Yeah. Actually, Bao Ding went in because of me."

"You can cut that bullshit out. In this line of work, people go in because of themselves."

Dunhuang smiled at her gratefully. "How old are you?"

"Fuck, don't you know you're not supposed to ask a woman's age?"

"Sorry. If I'm not supposed to ask, I won't ask."

"Guess."

"Twenty-two."

"You're even slicker than Bao Ding." Qibao took another cigarette from him. "Twenty-three. I can barely remember what that jerk Bao Ding looks like."

"He remembers you."

"Fuck, plenty of men remember me. Wouldn't you remember me?"

"Yes."

The corners of her mouth turned up in a smile. "Enough crap. What do you think of the food?"

"Pretty damn good." He meant it.

After dinner Dunhuang visited Qibao's place, so he'd know where it was. A two-bedroom apartment, Qibao in one room, another girl in the other. The apartment was small but nicely arranged, with a mattress, a television, a DVD player, speakers, and a little carpet. The blankets weren't folded. "It's messy," she said. "Don't look at the bed." He liked her directness. He looked at the bed, but didn't see anything in particular. He sized her up and thought that Qibao was just Bao Ding's style, no wonder he was worried about her. She made him a cup of instant coffee. The aroma of the coffee mixed with the smell of a woman's apartment made Dunhuang a little dizzy.

"The rent must be high," he said.

"It's okay. When you're alone in this city there's no one to spoil you, so you've got to spoil yourself."

Girls knew how to make the most out of life. He, on the other hand, had become a cheapskate. He consoled himself by saying that he had to be a cheapskate if he was ever going to get Bao Ding out of prison.

"Don't waste your time on rescue fantasies," she said when he mentioned this. "He'll be out in a year or two. He's getting three square meals, it won't kill him."

"That's not the point," Dunhuang said. "It's something I need to do, he went in because of me."

"Wow, so loyal!"

Before he'd finished the coffee, Qibao's phone rang. She looked at him, and he said, "No problem, I should be getting back anyway, I've got to pick up more movies."

Qibao said into the phone, Okay, I'll be there soon. Dunhuang said that if she wanted any DVDs she should help herself, and she picked out five, saying she'd return them after she'd watched them. She visited Zhongguancun often.

12

They met again two days later. Dunhuang was selling DVDs at Capital Normal University, and gave her a call—she was at home. They ate together, and this time Qibao treated. She returned the DVDs she'd borrowed and chose five new ones. Two people trying to get a foothold in Beijing had plenty to talk about. "Bao Ding told me to take care of you," joked Dunhuang. "Do you have any grunt work you need help with?"

"Grunt work is probably all you're good for," she said, "but it's not going to happen yet."

"I'll wait," he said. "Just call me when you want me." She reached out and patted him on both cheeks.

"Careful Bao Ding doesn't squash you when he gets out." They both laughed. They met next when Qibao came to Haidian to make a delivery and swung by Dunhuang's place to return the DVDs. It was nearing dusk, and Dunhuang had just gotten back. Huang, the student, wanted both the new and original versions of *Spring in a Small Town*, and Dunhuang was waiting for his call. Bored senseless, he was watching Japanese porn. When Qibao called his cellphone she was already at the west gate of Peking University. Dunhuang quickly shut off the DVD player and went to meet her.

She didn't think his little room was particularly ugly, and only complained that he didn't have so much as a glass of water to drink. Dunhuang ran to a nearby shop for some mineral water and green tea. The room was small, with one of them on the chair and the other on the bed their knees were practically touching. Dunhuang felt awkward—Qibao was wearing a skirt, and though it was a long one, he could still sense her skin every time their legs bumped. He was having trouble coming up with things to talk about. He told her to pick out a few more movies to borrow and had just opened his bag when Huang called, asking him to deliver his DVDs. Dunhuang asked Qibao to wait, he'd be right back.

Dunhuang jogged all the way to the dormitory building, where Huang was waiting to lead him upstairs. Some of his classmates had to write film criticism essays and needed DVDs. It took him more than half an hour to talk to everyone and write down the names of the movies they needed and then get back to his room. When he pushed open the door, Qibao let out a scream, fumbling with the remote in her hand, her face bright red. Dunhuang glanced at the TV screen and saw she had pressed the wrong button—instead of stopping the movie she'd paused it, and a naked man and woman were frozen in each other's arms on the screen. Mortified, Qibao threw the remote away from her. Dunhuang felt it was his responsibility to dispel her embarrassment, and as he picked up the remote from the floor he said,

"What are you screeching for, it's just porn! I was watching this earlier. Why don't we watch it together?"

"Piss off, I'm not watching that with you!" Qibao relaxed visibly.

"You'll regret it one day, once you're too old and worn out to bother."

Dunhuang parked himself with exaggerated nonchalance next to Qibao, and pressed play. She'd had it on mute, but he turned up the sound—he was going all in. Qibao sat motionless, and neither of them spoke. They sat frozen upright, staring at the screen, as though they'd lost the ability to turn their heads. The couple on the screen moved fluidly, their cries and moans swelling and fading, filling the small room. They sat on the edge of the bed like two slabs of marble, only gradually becoming aware of the other's breathing. Dunhuang moved a bit, Qibao moved a bit. Their knees touched. His heart in his throat, Dunhuang left his knee where it was, as though it had nothing to do with him. Then they slowly turned toward each other, eyes and faces on fire, and Qibao pulled him to her.

Qibao said, "Dunhuang. Dunhuang."

Dunhuang said, "Qibao. Qibao."

Then things got messy—as messy as they were onscreen. Qibao stripped with a speed that shocked Dunhuang, and even more shocking was what came next. "Wild" might describe it. He had no chance to use what he'd learned with Xiaorong—all that was too quiet, too proper, he was always one step behind. This was mano-a-mano. When she was on top Dunhuang felt as though a torrential river was raging over him—he completely forgot what he was supposed to be doing. Then, the river returned to earth and he was floating in softness, in abundance.

The onscreen tussle had also concluded, replaced by a pure, flat blue, as quiet as death.

Qibao patted his face and said, "You sure are young."

What the fuck did that mean?

"I made three or four hundred phone calls before I found you," said Dunhuang.

"Three or four hundred phone calls, just for this?" Qibao laughed, somewhat lewdly.

Dunhuang rolled off her. "Bao Ding told me to look after you."

"Could you not keep fucking bringing him up? He doesn't own me. We just slept together, it's nothing. What right does he have to tell you to look after me?" She sat up and started getting dressed.

"Are you leaving?" Dunhuang sat up too, and began retrieving her clothes from the floor. "I'll see you out."

"Are you trying to get rid of me?" Qibao said, tossing the clothes back on the floor. "I'm not leaving, I'm staying here tonight!"

And she meant it. They went out for dinner, and came back together. They watched an old Stephen Chow movie, *Hail the Judge*, then had another round in bed. In the late-night stillness, Qibao held Dunhuang. She said, "Holding you feels really solid."

"I'm skinny now," Dunhuang said. "If I were fatter it would feel even more solid."

"Shut up, you joker! I mean, when I hold you I feel anchored. Sometimes, when I'm alone, I can't cry, even when I want to. You know what I mean?"

"I hardly have time to laugh, why would I cry?"

"You men—you're stupid!"

"Why don't you just find someone to marry?"

"Oh it's that easy, is it?"

"Is it hard? If no one else is willing, I guess I could be convinced."

"Dream on! What about money? With you I'd be eating sand."

"That's true."

They didn't say anything else, and fell asleep in each others' arms. Dunhuang dreamed that Xiaorong was standing on a pedestrian overpass, shouting his name, the way he'd once shouted hers. Tears were streaming down her face as she called, and then she floated off the bridge like an old piece of clothing. Dunhuang woke covered in sweat. Qibao was sleeping soundly, her head in his armpit, smacking her lips lightly. Seen this way, eating even in her dreams, Qibao really looked only twenty-three. Dunhuang held her tightly. Just like she'd said—he wanted to cry but couldn't.

Dunhuang tried not to think about Bao Ding. Restock. Sell DVDs. Call Qibao when he missed her. When she wanted to come over he'd go home and wait there. When she wanted him to come out he'd put down whatever he was doing and run or take the bus to where she was. His routines were regular but hers weren't—it was impossible for a fake ID seller to have routines. She had a lot of friends she went carousing with, and she came home at all hours—sometimes, when he called at midnight, she was still out. He urged her to be careful, it wasn't safe for a girl to come home too late by herself. She said she'd be happier dead anyway.

He had been sorting DVDs when she said that. "That's a nice way to talk. What if you were assaulted?"

"Do you mean for money or for sex?"

"What do you think?"

"If they're after money I don't have any. If they're after sex…well it's about time to start shopping around, anyway."

"You're determined to drive me crazy!"

Qibao was intently painting her toenails black, and didn't even look up. "Look at you, worried about this, worried about that. Even if no one else drives you crazy you'll do it to yourself."

That made Dunhuang pause, and he put down what he was doing. He was fucking twenty-five years old—when had he become such a nag? But after he berated himself he couldn't help adding, "But seriously, how about we rent a place together? You could quit the ID business—they're coming down harder on it lately."

"Hell no," Qibao said, kicking her legs in the air. "You stay in your place, I'll stay in mine. I'm not interested in controlling anyone, and I sure as hell don't want to be in anyone else's pocket."

"Look at where you're living—that girl's screeches are horrible." Dunhuang was talking about the roommate. One night, Qibao told him to come over because her roommate wasn't going to be home. He went, but in the middle of the night the girl came back after all, and brought a guy with her. Then it was shouting and moaning all night, as though she'd brought back a dozen guys—Dunhuang hadn't slept a wink.

"God, so she yells a bit when she's happy, what's wrong with that? Not everyone's like you, plowing away in silence."

Dunhuang held his peace, watching Qibao minister to her toes. "I just care about you. You're my girlfriend, after all."

"Whoo! Lucky me." She continued applying nail polish.

It was hopeless.

Back to sorting. His hand paused over *The Bicycle Thief*, as he thought of the girl in Zhichunli. He hadn't heard from her in days. He remembered the last time she called was three days after he'd given her *The Bicycle Thief*. She said she watched it. She wanted another violent movie and another horror, and two of something else while he was at it. He asked, What something else? She said, something like *The Bicycle Thief*. He asked her if she liked it, and she suddenly said she'd have to call back later, someone was at the door. About five minutes later she called again, saying sorry, but that she was busy, and she would call again some other time. Then she hung up. Dunhuang had waited, but she never called again. He waited a few more days, then tried calling a couple of times, but she never picked up. Then he'd found Qibao, and was too distracted to think of the girl again.

He worked it out—seventeen days. It wasn't normal. He dialed her number, and she still didn't answer. He decided to go have a look, and asked Qibao if she wanted to go.

"Go where?" she asked.

"To see a girl."

"Is she pretty?"

"Of course."

"Then I'll go, to keep an eye on you."

When he said he was running there she complained, "It's on the other side of Zhongguancun, are you nuts? If you can't afford the bus I'll pay for it."

"Forget it then, you can stay home."

Qibao grumbled for a while, then said, "Okay, I guess misery loves company."

Dunhuang briefly explained the girl's situation, then they were out the door and moving. As they passed Pacific Computer City Qibao began running out of steam. They managed to stagger across the Zhongguancun bridge, but then Qibao plopped herself down on the street and refused to move, insisting they get a taxi. She wouldn't go back, and wouldn't let him keep running. Misery loves company indeed. Dunhuang had no choice but to get a taxi. "You're crazy," she said, once they were in the cab.

They buzzed up from downstairs, but no one answered. "Stop flattering yourself," said Qibao. "She's ignoring you." Dunhuang wouldn't give up, however, and waited by the door.

At last someone went in, and they went in after. They climbed to the top floor, and saw two wide white strips of paper pasted over the girl's door. Qibao looked at him with satisfaction, "See? You're being gallant for nothing."

"What the hell do you know," Dunhuang said. "Why would her apartment suddenly be sealed?"

"Ask the police department."

Dunhuang stood in front of the door for a while, trying to peer through the peephole, but it was blocked. He was baffled. Qibao dragged him back downstairs. He sat down on the steps outside the door and insisted on having a cigarette. As he was lighting it, a middle-aged woman came downstairs, and he asked her if she knew why the apartment on the top floor had been sealed. The woman shook her head, saying she didn't know, and went on her way. He asked another person passing by, who had even less of a clue.

"What's going on?" asked Qibao. "Why are you so concerned?"

"I just want to know what she thought of the movie I gave her."

"You mean *The Bicycle Thief*? That's it?"

"What else could it be? If I disappeared one day—no body, no nothing—what would you think?"

"An asshole like you, you're sure to have run off with some girl!"

"Wouldn't you be sad?"

"What fucking good would that do? Who knows why people disappear, what if it's something good? Maybe the apartment wasn't sealed because of her, but because of someone else. For instance, she could be the mistress of a corrupt official or a rich businessman's concubine, and she got tired of the cushy life."

"But what if she was depressed or agoraphobic, and something bad happened?"

"Whoa, 'agoraphobic'—did you get a master's degree behind my back? She's probably depress-a-phobic because she can't spend all her money!"

"Yeah, probably so." Dunhuang stood and glanced up at the windows on the top floor. After a while he said, "'Mistress'…'concubine'…can't you be a little more positive?"

"What's wrong with mistresses and concubines? Plenty of people would jump at the chance."

It wasn't an argument worth having, so Dunhuang ignored her—he thought she was the one being brainless now. Qibao saw he was giving her the cold shoulder so she did the same in return. They took a cab in silence back toward Weixiuyuan. As they were passing Zhongguancun, Qibao said she wanted to stop and get yogurt.

"Okay," said Dunhuang, "let's have the driver drop us off at the supermarket." The fight was over.

13

That night, Dunhuang had another dream like the last one. Xiaorong shouting his name as she floated off the bridge. It was all perfectly clear in his dream, as though he were in a slow-motion scene in a film, too slow for him to grab her. Just before Xiaorong reached the ground, her face became that of the girl in Zhichunli. Dunhuang awoke scared. He'd never been superstitious, but something struck him as wrong about the sealing of the Zhichunli apartment. And that dream was strange. But what could he do? The next morning, as soon as he woke up, he called Xiaorong. She was distant at first, but she soon sounded normal. "What's up," she asked, throwing the ball immediately in his court.

He hemmed and hawed, then said, "I just wanted to tell you, I found Qibao."

"You found her, that's great!" she said. "That's great. Bring her over to meet me, let's do it today."

Dunhuang decided he'd spring for dinner at Ancients. Qibao didn't want to go, saying meeting his "adopted sister" was like meeting the family, but he finally convinced her, as a favor to him.

It was the same table as last time. Xiaorong saw them the

moment she walked in, and was quietly surprised by Qibao's beauty. Kuang Shan came in after, and only noticed her as they approached the table. He stopped and pointed his finger at her, appearing to be deep in thought. "You…We've met before."

Qibao stood up and said, "Yes, we had dinner together once."

"Right, that's right, with a bunch of friends. What's your name? I guess Beijing's still way too small," Kuang Shan said.

"So this is Qibao," said Xiaorong. "She's awfully pretty, and so young!"

"Hi Xiaorong," said Qibao. "Dunhuang's always saying nice things about you."

"About me?" Xiaorong started laughing. "What's there to say! I'm practically an old maid."

"You are not!" said Dunhuang.

Qibao chimed in, "You have real elegance, just the kind of feminine maturity that men like. That's not something that ages!"

"I'm afraid it does," replied Xiaorong. "This one's practically lost interest in me."

Qibao pointed at Kuang Shan. "You ought to be ashamed of yourself, thinking the grass is greener."

Kuang Shan waved this off. "I certainly don't! I've hardly even looked over the fence."

"Waiter, we're ready to order," Dunhuang said. "A half-and-half spicy pot, two plates of winter melon, and two plates of mushrooms. You guys order the rest."

The pot boiled, and roiling steam cut off Dunhuang from Xiaorong. Though neither of them felt any danger in staying silent, they still kept the conversation going, avoiding awkward pauses. Dunhuang talked to Kuang Shan about the DVD trade, while Xiaorong waxed solicitous about how Qibao was getting along in Beijing, then moved on to cosmetics and snack food—conversation was livelier than they'd feared. Halfway through the meal, however, Kuang Shan had to leave—business at the shop, they'd been doing inventory. Dunhuang urged him to stay, but Xiaorong said, "Let him go if he needs to go, they're waiting for him at the shop." The three of them continued eating, and she said, "Qibao, have some more, should we get some tofu strips?" Qibao's youth was most evident in the way she ate: head down, chopsticks flying, picking out her favorites. As she was absorbed in the food her phone rang, she went out to take the call and didn't come back for nearly ten minutes. When she did, she said a friend was having a birthday party, and had asked her to go right over.

"Can't you wait a bit?" said Dunhuang. "At least finish eating."

"I've got to go," she said, rubbing her hand over the stubble on Dunhuang's scalp. "Next time I'll treat Xiaorong, how's that? You can come along too."

"Go on, Qibao," said Xiaorong. "You ought to be there for the party. We'll have plenty of chances to hang out."

Then there were two. Dunhuang was a little annoyed; the wheels had completely fallen off the dinner. "Jesus, the whole world has something better to do, I'm the only one sitting on his thumbs. Let's keep eating."

"No big deal. Another couple beers? I've already forgotten what you're like when you're drunk."

Dunhuang drank glass after glass in silence. At around eleven he took her back to her building. Xiaorong asked, "Do you want to come up for a glass of water? He's been staying at the shop these days." Dunhuang went up.

There were fewer DVDs in the room this time, and many of the baskets were empty and stacked. She said they'd all been taken to the store for inventory. Dunhuang nodded, feeling a little dizzy—not a surprise considering how much he'd drunk.

"Qibao's pretty nice," said Xiaorong.

"Thanks," Dunhuang said, looking at her. Xiaorong turned her face away, toward the hot-water thermos. "Oh, I was going to get you some water." She picked up the cup that Dunhuang had used while he was staying there, packed it with tea leaves and poured the water. "Strong tea clears the head." She held out the cup, but Dunhuang took her hand. She said, "Dunhuang…" The cup fell to the ground and he pulled her into his arms. She said, "We can't do this."

"Do what?" Dunhuang said.

Dunhuang only held her, nothing else. "I dreamed you jumped off a bridge," he said. "You drifted down like a piece of clothing. Scared me awake." Xiaorong's voice was low. "My life is just fine, why would I die?" She pulled Dunhuang's head down to her chest. Dunhuang felt even dizzier and his ears buzzed. They collapsed sideways onto the bed. The place was too damn small. Xiaorong said, "We can't, Dunhuang, I've got…"

"So do I!" Dunhuang said.

He put his mouth and tongue between Xiaorong's chin and neck. It was the softest part of her. Her only protest was deep in her throat, she sounded like she might cry. Slowly, her arms and legs opened to him, then she contracted and began to shudder. Dunhuang was already inside her, but she was silent. She only ever flowed on the ground, she never raged in the sky, like Qibao did.

As Xiaorong stuffed the pillow cover into her mouth and bit down, Dunhuang was coming as well. As he worked, he reached for the shelf at the head of the bed—he had to get a condom on soon. Xiaorong pulled the cover from her mouth and said, "Don't bother, I'm pregnant."

Dunhuang stopped.

"I found out two days ago."

Dunhuang stayed motionless, and the name "Kuang Xia" flashed in his head. The blood ebbed from where it had gathered, vanishing as quickly as the cup of water he'd just drunk. He was gradually losing sensation, losing shape and volume, until he finally drifted from her body like a wisp of smoke.

The sound of night trucks passing by the window. A dull explosion from somewhere nearby, and the sound of car alarms going off. Later, all sound faded away, and the night was still but for the ticking of the bedside clock.

"I shouldn't have asked you to come up."

"What are you going to do?"

"Do I have any choice?"

"You'll keep it?"

"I'll keep it. I can't get rid of it. It's my child, it's part of my body."

"So get married, have the kid, and live in Beijing?"

"I'll take it one day at a time. It's the only thing in this place that belongs to me."

Dunhuang immediately thought of all those women who sold DVDs and ID cards with babies in tow, their shirts open and nursing in public as they asked, Want a DVD? Need an ID? Xiaorong got dressed and walked to the bathroom, looking lonely and abandoned with her shirt hanging askew. Dunhuang imagined that she was walking not toward the toilet but toward the street, children appearing on her back and in her arms. She sat down at the curbside and hiked up her shirt, stifling the cries of a child named Kuang Xia with one large, white breast. Dunhuang lit a cigarette. Xiaorong emerged from the bathroom, her clothes tidied and hair combed, and said, "Don't smoke in here, it's bad for the baby." Dunhuang obediently pinched it out, and thought it might not be as bad as he imagined. Perhaps she'd spend her days sitting in state in the Cosmic DVD shop, smiling at all the customers, gracefully counting their earnings. Who knew?

Dunhuang left the room on the pretense of wanting another cigarette. He didn't go back. As he left the building he looked up at the windows, most of which were dark, and no faces showed in the ones that were lit. *That's good*, thought Dunhuang. *It's best this way.*

14

At last, spring had truly arrived. But Beijing's springs are short—yawn and you'll miss them, and the next day will hit 28 degrees Celsius while you're still wearing your sweater. The novelty had begun to wear off for Dunhuang and Qibao, too—they each dealt with their own lives, focused on their own business, and didn't see each other as much as before. Qibao was still refusing to move in with him, and told him to quit pushing or she'd dump him. So Dunhuang continued to live in his little room in Weixiuyuan, and thought that was fine—if he had to piss in the middle of the night he could just do it on the scholar tree. He thought he might be personally responsible for some of the tree's new leaves.

Dunhuang gave Qibao a key to his room so she could come over when he wasn't home. When she was bored she would show up with some junk food and watch DVDs until Dunhuang got back. Then she might do his laundry, but she wasted so much water the landlady developed a facial tic just watching her, since utilities were included in the rent. She couldn't come right out and complain, instead she tried an oblique approach, "My goodness, you've been at those two shirts so long, I thought you were washing ten at least."

Qibao immediately knew what she was getting at. When she'd first arrived in Beijing she'd stayed in a place just like this one, where the landlord was constantly at her to use fifteen-watt bulbs, and telling her, "Don't expect to make anything worth eating in those electric rice cookers, what you need is a coal stove, buy a coal stove." Qibao wasn't having any of it, and six months later the landlord drove her out. *This old bag*, thought Qibao, *she's even a cheapskate about the water.*

"Well you know, ma'am, Dunhuang was a poor child, he's only got these two shirts, and he wears them one after the other. He's as filthy as a metalworker and it takes a lot of work to get them clean. The sheets are worse."

The landlady's heart nearly broke. Sheets, too... There wouldn't be enough water in the whole Yangtze river, the water meter was sure to burn out altogether. "That Dunhuang sure is lucky," she said, "to have a girlfriend as good as you."

"You flatter me," Qibao said, with secret satisfaction. "Laundry is about all I can do. It's easy, as long as you use plenty of water."

Later, after Qibao left, the landlady paced the yard, wondering how to raise the rent. She went to look once again at the water meter, and when she came back she noticed the light was on in the room. She pushed her way inside and saw the bed covered in DVDs. "What's this?" She pointed at the bed.

"Movies," said Dunhuang.

"No, they're DVDs, pirated DVDs. Where'd you get them?"

"I bought them."

"What'd you buy so many for?"

"To sell them."

"Oh, you sell pirated DVDs." The landlady's finger shifted to him. "So you've been breaking the law!"

"It's not really illegal, ma'am," Dunhuang said. "The streets are full of them. They're in all the shops."

"Piracy is illegal! I'm a Party secretary, you can't fool me! And you also lied about being a graduate student!"

"I never said that, you did."

"I did? How would I have known if you didn't tell me?"

Dunhuang couldn't be bothered to argue, and started packing up his things. "Ma'am, if there's something you want to say, then say it."

"All right then, I'll be direct. I can't let a seller of pirated DVDs live in my house, and for only four hundred and fifty kuai! If the police knew about it, this old face would be lost completely. I'm a Party secretary!"

"How much extra?"

"One hundred."

Dunhuang looked at her. He slapped the wall. "Ma'am, the lease isn't even up yet, do you think it's reasonable to raise the rent? Also, before it's completely dark, go and take a look at this place from the outside. If you still think it's worth that much, come back in for the money."

She really was a secretary—she switched strategies instantly. "It's not the money I'm concerned about, it's my reputation. I can't just invite any old lawbreaker into my home. If you think it's too expensive you can leave. It's not hard to find lodgers around Zhongguancun and Peking University."

"You think students will rent from you? They're putting up new dorms at Peking University all the time, everyone lives in high rises now, just one thousand twenty kuai a year! The student apartments in Wanliu used to be bursting, now they're full of tumbleweeds."

"You're just fooling me."

"I'm an applicant for the doctorate program at Peking

University, you better believe I did my homework. Forget it, I'm not arguing with you. I'll add fifty, take it or leave it. I can move out tomorrow."

The landlady left, but knocked on the door again a little later. Dunhuang said, "It's open." She said she wouldn't come in. She'd just called her daughter, who urged her to take pity on a single man in the city. She could accept a little less—fifty was fine. Starting the next month, and not to forget. "Stingy bitch," mumbled Dunhuang.

"What did you say?" the landlady asked.

"I said I'll soon be rich," answered Dunhuang.

When Dunhuang told Qibao, she said, "If it had been me, I would have had it out with the old hag, at worst you find a new place to live. In a city this size how hard could that be? Goddammit, if I ever have money I'll build a hundred apartment buildings, fifty stories at least, and rent them all out. Then I'll sit at home all day and count my cash."

"If you can't count it all I'll help you."

"That's all you're good for—sitting at home! Why can't you just say, 'fuck it, I'm going out to earn rent for you?' Grow a spine—hey, I'm talking to you!" She whacked him on the shoulder. It hurt a bit. "You see? A little smack and you stare like an idiot. You go around looking like the weight of the world is on your shoulders."

Dunhuang stopped short, as though he'd been stung by a wasp. She was right. When had he started worrying so much about other people's rotten business? What had happened to that expansive sense of him-against-the-world he'd had when he first got out of jail? Back then he'd scoffed at Beijing: worst come to worst he could always sleep under a bridge, could always beg for a meal, begging wasn't a crime. What had happened to that sense of taking each day as it came, of not having a care in the world? Back then, women were nothing to him: nice if you could get them, but to hell with them if you couldn't. As long as he wasn't under lock and key, life was good. When had life suddenly gotten so complicated? When had he started fretting? Jesus Christ.

"Fuck, are you meditating again?" Qibao poked his cheek. "You're either staring at the wall or you're catching flies in your mouth, how the hell did I ever fall for you? Now you're having an out-of-body experience—wake up!"

"I want to go visit Bao Ding."

"So go, you don't need to notify me."

"Will you go with me?"

"No." She started putting on her sneakers. "What am I going to tell him—that we've been sleeping together?"

"So don't go."

"Fine, I won't."

That night, they went to the Old Summer Palace, climbing over the wall in a small alley. They'd done it with a group of friends a few nights before, but had only stayed half an hour. Qibao hadn't had her fill, and dragged Dunhuang back again. He boosted her over the wall, hands on her ass, and they heard the frogs croaking before they'd even reached Fu Lake. "Damn it's big," said Qibao. "Those Qing dynasty pigs really knew how to enjoy themselves." The night-silence in the Summer Palace had a weight to it that pressed down on the surface of Fu Lake. Dunhuang was a little surprised at Qibao's guts, running around happily in the pitch-black park, making a show of playing the tour guide for Dunhuang, explaining which palace girl had died here, or which eunuch had been executed there. Wronged ghosts everywhere. As they neared the ruins of the great fountains Dunhuang was getting goose bumps, but Qibao was perfectly unconcerned, ducking among the ruined walls and uttering strange bird-like cries. The sound was gentler than a crow's cawing, and terribly eerie. Then she laughed. Dunhuang told her to keep quiet or she'd have the park guards on them. Later, tired, she lay down on a broken slab of stone and told him to lay down next to her. She said if the stone wasn't so chilly they could sleep there, and leave by the front gate in the morning. Dunhuang assented, and rolled over on top of her.

"Don't get frisky, look where we are!"

"I couldn't get frisky if I wanted to, I think it's frozen off completely." Dunhuang kissed her. "There's something I want to ask you."

"As long as it's not about money."

"Old married couples can't stand on ceremony. If a man borrows money he'll repay it!"

"A man shouldn't have to borrow money!" Qibao held Dunhuang close, her eyes wide as she said, "You've got a one-track mind. I told you, give up on 'saving' Bao Ding. Even if you sold the two of us it wouldn't do the trick. If two or three thousand was enough I'd have put it up long ago. Do you have any connections? You're not going to meet Buddha just by lighting incense!"

"Well I need to meet him somehow! I can't just stand here while someone rots away because of me."

"Because of you? It's because of money! Anyone who does our work is going to jail eventually, it's just a matter of time."

"I can't explain it to you," Dunhuang said, pushing her arms away and rolling off her. "You women will never understand men's business."

"It was women that squeezed you fucking men out, what's so hard to understand? You're just a typical Neanderthal, you can never be wrong. Why can't you just save the money up, and then give it to him when he gets out? He'll need it more then than he does now."

Dunhuang rolled back on top of her. "Damn, ball-and-chain, that's good thinking. That's exactly how I felt when I'd just gotten out and had no cash."

"Piss off," Qibao said, pushing him away. "I came to Beijing when I was eighteen; what mud puddle were you playing in back then?"

"I was trying to pass my tests, studying molecular formulas. Hydrogen plus oxygen is water."

"Wow, you should be a college professor."

"I thought so, too, but they didn't want me."

Qibao started laughing. "You're full of yourself right up to the eyebrows." Dunhuang laughed too. This damned girl had to have been squeezed out by a fox spirit, not another woman. No question.

15

Qibao bought Dunhuang a whole new set of clothes; from every angle he looked like a proper gentleman. She said, "You *ought* to look like a proper gentleman, both for yourself and for Bao Ding, you don't want the prison guards to die laughing." Besides cigarettes he brought a bite to eat, anything more and Bao Ding would have no place to keep it, and he wouldn't be permitted to keep it anyway. He also brought a little medicine—Bao Ding had stomach problems—and some cash. When he got there, Bao Ding would tell him which guards to give it to. Dunhuang couldn't even be sure Bao Ding was still in the same place. If he'd been moved, Dunhuang would have to make another trip.

The guard at the gate didn't remember Dunhuang. There was no need to explain himself, he just passed some cigarettes to the police who'd brought him, and was taken in to see the head of the prison, where he handed out more smokes. They checked, Bao Ding was still there. Then he was following a guard through rooms and corridors that he still recognized. The place hadn't changed in the past few months, neither had the faces and expressions of the guards—even the half-footprint on the wall where the corridor turned was still there.

The grass in the prison yard was shining slickly, and moss was starting to appear on the shaded stone steps. The riflemen in the watchtowers cradled their guns, gazing into the distance. Dunhuang heard many people shouting slogans in unison, and the sound of marching footsteps like countless knives chopping vegetables. He was able to distinguish that sound from the general stillness of the yard, something he had never been able to do before: back then, he'd either been locked up in silence, or he'd been part of the vegetable-chopping brigade. You only ever heard one thing: either silence, or chopping.

"Wait here," said the guard.

Dunhuang sat on a nearby chair. He was in a big room fitted with an iron barrier and thick glass, like you'd see on TV—always looking a little different, but feeling the same. A while later he heard someone say, "Go in!" and Bao Ding came in through a door on the other side of the barrier. He'd lost a lot of weight.

Dunhuang stood up. "Hey, man."

"I guessed it was you, Dunhuang." Bao Ding sat down across from him, starting to grin but then stopping himself. His face was a mass of bruises, and there were scabs at the corner of mouth and eye. "Nice duds, are they new? A man ought to look good."

"Your face…" Dunhuang glanced at the guard five meters off.

"It's nothing. Got into a fight with a Hubei guy. Cocksucker was messing with a friend and I got sick of it, got into it with him. It's almost better."

"How's your hand?"

"That's fine—I wouldn't have taken on the Hubei punk otherwise."

"I thought I might not be able to find you."

"I think they're transferring me soon, they can't keep me here past seven months without charging me. How are you doing?"

"Not bad, I'm selling DVDs. I haven't gotten together enough money yet," he said, lowering his voice, and his head.

"Are you nuts? I told you before, don't even think about it. I know what's what, even if I'm convicted it's only a year or two, I'll survive. Don't kill yourself on my account. I've got room and board, you worry about yourself. Just bring me a carton of smokes from time to time."

"I brought some. Also some food and stuff, stomach pills." Dunhuang lowered his voice again. "And something to grease palms with, if you need it."

"Either way, it's cool," Bao Ding said. "Did you find Qibao?"

"Yeah, she helped me buy all this stuff. Picked out these clothes, too. She's been busy lately, so she couldn't come with me."

As he spoke, Dunhuang stared at a smudge on the glass, thinking it was probably year-old fly shit. Silence seemed to spread outward from his own ears, then he heard Bao Ding say, "She's not bad, huh?"

"Yeah, she's nice."

Bao Ding started laughing, then put a hand to his face and stopped. "It's fine," he said. "Don't worry about it, I'm a big boy. Just concentrate on making money."

"Okay."

"Remember, whatever happens, don't let it get to you."

"Okay."

"Go on back."

"Okay."

They finished before their visiting time was up. Dunhuang watched Bao Ding being taken back through the door, walking stiffly, the scraping of his shoes on the concrete a little chilling. Go on back, he'd said, as easy as that. Qibao. Qibao. Dunhuang looked at the empty doorway, and silently cursed Qibao—*You know what, you really are the child of a fox spirit.* The guard yelled, "He's gone!" and Dunhuang realized he was still sitting there dumbly. He quickly stood.

He took it upon himself to do a little palm-greasing on his own, and was a long time about it. Standing outside the prison gates, smoking, he was totally exhausted. By the time he paid for the bus to get back to the city he was nearly penniless.

The sun went down as the bus reached Hangtian Bridge. Dunhuang got off and headed for Qibao's place. Her phone was off, she was most likely asleep. She distinguished night from day not by the clock or by the sun, but by when she felt sleepy. Whenever she was sleepy it was night; the sun could be shining, but she'd pull the curtains and crash. She was a savage, fearless little creature, going her own way. Dunhuang rang the bell downstairs over and over, but no one answered. Fuck, she was a deep sleeper. He rang again, and finally someone answered the intercom—Qibao's roommate, the girl with legs as skinny as chopsticks. Qibao called her Bony Beauty, but Dunhuang thought The Skeleton was more like it. Plenty of go in that skinny body, though, she was always bringing men home with her. Dunhuang didn't see the appeal of lying on top of a rack of ribs.

"Who's trying to break the buzzer," Bony Beauty said nastily. Dunhuang announced himself, and her tone softened a bit. "Qibao's not here." He asked where she'd gone, and the girl said she didn't know, try asking her cellphone.

"Try asking her cellphone"—nice. Would I be here if that had worked? Dunhuang assumed she was pissed off because she'd had to push some guy off her to answer the intercom. Just

hanging around seemed boring, so he went to the supermarket, bought a pack of stickers, and started making ads. He changed the wording: "All movies, any movies." Once he'd finished, he started pasting them nearby, choosing quiet corners and unobtrusive spots. The sanitation workers were campaigning against advertising like his, calling it "urban psoriasis," and posting stickers in obvious places was just asking to have them torn down. He stuck some on the mailboxes in the lobby of the apartment building. It was nine thirty by the time he was done, and Qibao's phone was still off. He was starving, so he went to Malan Noodles for a bowl of something, then took his time sauntering back. She still wasn't home. This time Bony Beauty didn't snap at him, but said, "I'm sure she'll be back any minute, want to come up and wait?"

Dunhuang said he'd stay downstairs, he was afraid he'd have to listen to Bony Beauty's caterwauling. He sat down on a low wall in the garden outside the building, put his head on his knees, and was asleep in two minutes, his body a rigid triangle. When he woke it was one in the morning and Qibao was standing in front of him, reeking of booze. "What are you doing here?"

Dunhuang stood, his bones creaking. He felt a nameless indignation gathering in his gut. "Where else should I be?"

"I'm sorry, I didn't know you were coming. I went out with friends."

"What the hell kind of friends don't need to sleep at night?"

"Just drinking buddies okay? Here, help me upstairs." Qibao made to take his arm. Dunhuang shook it off, saying, "I'm not fucking going anywhere!"

"Keep your voice down."

"Why should I keep my voice down!?" Dunhuang was

shouting, a little hysterically, "What the fuck is everybody sleeping for? Wake the hell up!"

Lights came on in several windows, and heads poked out: "Who's yelling? Let us sleep, you asshole!"

Dunhuang pointed at them and shouted: "You're the fucking assholes!"

"What's wrong with you!" said Qibao. "Come upstairs!"

"I'm not fucking going," said Dunhuang, then turned and started walking off. Qibao called after him but he ignored her, lengthening his stride. Qibao followed him out of the compound onto the street, saying: "Dunhuang, if you don't stop this instant I'll kill you so help me God!"

Dunhuang stopped. "Go ahead then. Kill me now."

Qibao walked around in front of him and saw that he was crying. She softened, handing him a tissue to wipe his face. "I know you're upset about Bao Ding," she said. "I really did go have dinner with friends tonight, and my phone battery died this afternoon. Cross my heart."

Dunhuang lit a cigarette, his heart choked with weeds. "Go back home," he said to her, then started walking. He didn't know what Bao Ding would have done if it was he who'd been let out, and Dunhuang was still inside. He smoked one cigarette after another, tossing the butts aside. Qibao followed behind him, picking up each butt he tossed, and in that way they eventually arrived at Suzhou Bridge. More than an hour of walking—she hadn't walked so much in all her years in Beijing. Her feet were aching; she felt she couldn't take another step. She flagged a taxi on the night shift, and pulled up alongside Dunhuang.

"Get in," she said, showing him her handful of cigarette butts. "If you want to keep up this stupid act, you can forget about seeing me again."

Dunhuang looked at the cigarette butts in her hand—thirty in all. He opened the cab door and got in.

16

May brought another sandstorm. The weather forecast called it a historical anomaly. But it came all the same. A day and night of roaring gales, sending sands into the sky. Women wore high-necked sweaters to keep the dust out of their cleavage; men turned their collars up and perched sunglasses on their noses. Rarely was May in Beijing so grave and humorless. Then the winds ceased, like a hundred-meter sprinter halting in his tracks, too sudden for the Meteorology Bureau to keep up. The fine sand hung in the air, turning heaven and earth a dusky yellow, and the pollution indicators went through the roof. The news instructed everyone to stay indoors, and to good effect—Dunhuang worked every day, but even in the sheltered corners sold no more than a couple of DVDs. Sales this poor were unusual, but then again maybe not unlikely—once again there was word of a clampdown, and this time it seemed real. Dunhuang wandered past the police station and saw none of the usual banners—"Protect Intellectual Copyright," "Crush Piracy," "Rectify the Audio-Visual Market"—but he was nevertheless circumspect, and for a few days posted no advertisements. Two days prior, he'd been selling DVDs when a young guy with a backpack had come running past, and when he saw Dunhuang he shouted, Run! They're making arrests! Dunhuang knew him, a good guy, whenever they met they'd have a chat. Dunhuang believed him, and within five seconds had his DVDs in his bag and his bag on his back. He overtook the other guy, and when he looked back after 800 meters or so saw neither him nor the police. Dunhuang wondered whether he'd been played for a fool, but he never ran into the guy after that.

The DVDs sold grudgingly, he hadn't restocked for a week. The floating dust was eventually brought down with iodide-induced artificial rain, and the sky was once again high and blue. Dunhuang counted his movies, and decided it was time to pay Cosmic a visit.

From across the street, Cosmic looked the same as before, except for two crossed strips of tape over the door. The date on the notice was from two days prior. Dunhuang stood in front of the door, empty pack on his back, weighing his cellphone in his hand. Xiaorong, Kuang Shan…he thought about who to call, and settled on Kuang Shan. Kuang Shan sounded like an anxious old man on the phone, though he relaxed when he realized it was Dunhuang.

"Brother, I'm fucked."

Kuang Shan said he'd only just gotten out of the detention center that morning—Xiaorong had needed all the money in the house to get him out. Who would have thought that the police would show up in the middle of the day and push their way past the curtain into the rear storage room. All the pirated DVDs were there, tied in bundles and stacked on the shelves. It was fully stocked—if it hadn't been for the sandstorm they would have been nearly sold out. Every last DVD was confiscated, they'd arrived with a small van. The van had already been partially filled—clearly Cosmic had not been their first stop of the day. The beeline they made for the curtained back room indicated their familiarity with DVD shops. Given the shocking price of authorized movies, no shop could survive without pirated stock. Luckily, most of the pornography was still under the bed at his house or he never would have gotten out so easily. Kuang Shan and Boss Zhou had been taken together. Both were out now, thanks to payments from family members, of course.

"So what now?" asked Dunhuang.

"Got to catch our breath first," said Kuang Shan. "Want to stop by for a drink?"

"Sure. How's Xiaorong?"

"She took it better than me. Women just make no sense. She used to go on and on about earning enough to go back home, but now that we're broke she isn't saying a thing, like it was someone else's money to begin with. I have to say I feel bad for putting her through all this... You must be ready to restock?"

"Yeah, I'm about out."

"Talk to a guy named Boss Feng, tell him I sent you. Don't tell anyone what happened, okay?"

Dunhuang followed his directions to a little restaurant called The Great Swan, and a bearded man met him at the door, saying Kuang Shan had called ahead. He said Boss Feng was out of town and had sent him instead. The DVDs were a few minutes away, in a sort of underground parking garage. Dunhuang followed the beard downstairs and through at least eight winding turns before they arrived at Boss Feng's "shop." It was essentially one big trash dump, with DVDs everywhere. The floor was entirely covered in the garish colors of packages and the silver glints of unpackaged discs; everyone inside simply walked over them. It was more DVDs than Dunhuang had ever seen in his life—a space of probably one hundred square meters filled with mountains of DVDs. It was practically a DVD factory. Seeing Dunhuang's open mouth, the beard casually remarked that this was one of their smaller shops and the selection was limited, he should just pick out what he could use.

This is a real fucking eye-opener, Dunhuang thought as he rummaged. He suddenly seemed laughable to himself—a little clown of a DVD peddler. He filled his backpack and a suitcase then dragged them laboriously across the mountains of movies, feeling even more silly. One pack and one suitcase, only a drop in the bucket to these guys. Kuang Shan must have felt the same way in the beginning, but at least it drove him to open his own shop.

The prices at Boss Feng's were even cheaper than Cosmic, and Dunhuang continued to restock there. The clampdown was continuing and he kept a low profile on the streets, out of the sights of the police and city management. Every few days he made the rounds to his old customers: the PKU dorms, the office building at Changhong bridge, and a few other places—in and out, wherever he saw an opening. He continued to get a few calls from old customers as well. If something didn't feel right he just stayed at home, or went out shopping with Qibao. Or he'd accompany her on deliveries, though things were bad for the fake ID business, too, and her work came in fits and starts. Things between them were good one moment, bad the next—good when they were together, bad when one of them disappeared. But Qibao preferred that to going around joined at the hip.

He still hadn't gone for a drink with Kuang Shan; he didn't feel like listening to his woes. Kuang Shan had called him once to tell him that Xiaorong's belly was starting to show. Laying on his bed and imagining what that must look like, Dunhuang was even less inclined to visit. After a few days of "catching his breath," Kuang Shan started selling DVDs with Xiaorong. They would start from square one, he said, and Cosmic would rise again. Dunhuang spotted him at the gate of the Forestry University. He'd been planning to sell DVDs there, but when he saw Kuang Shan he stayed on the bus and kept going.

Life was dull for quite some time. The weather was hot, and it was uncomfortable both indoors and out. Outside, the sun scorched him until he was short of breath. Inside, the heat seemed to pass straight through the brick walls and concrete roof. He was uneasy, it felt like something was about to happen. And then something did.

It was noon and he was drinking beer in a small restaurant outside of Weixiuyuan when the phone rang. The caller's voice sounded strange and he wouldn't reveal who he was, only asking where Dunhuang was. When Dunhuang told him the "West Gate Chicken Wing" joint, the caller hung up. Apprehensive, he rushed to pay the bill and leave, but at the door found someone blocking his way. When he looked up his mouth dropped open—it was Bao Ding.

"Going somewhere?" Bao Ding said with a grin.

"You scared the crap out of me, I thought it was a sting!" Dunhuang turned and yelled to the server, "Bring a menu, we're ordering!" She was in the midst of clearing his table, and looked at him blankly. "Something wrong with your ears?" he said. "Ten bottles of beer!"

They sat down, and Dunhuang asked, "Why didn't you tell me you were getting out?"

"Didn't know myself," Bao Ding answered. He guzzled

an entire bottle of chilled beer, then belched once and farted twice before continuing. "Remember last time I told you I got into a fight inside, protecting some other guy? Well that guy was from Changping, he was in for knocking up some girl he shouldn't have. Turns out his big brother's some kind of official. Anyway, he had some strings to pull, and the brother got the guy sprung. I was included in the deal and came out with him—he's a stand-up guy."

"You don't blame me, do you?" Dunhuang asked.

Bao Ding punched his shoulder. "You're messed up in the head, kid! What the hell is that guy to me? He's got a political background—at most I'll be buddy-buddy with him over a few drinks, and that's it. You and I aren't like that, we don't count for shit—there won't even be headstones on our graves! Why would I blame you? If I did I wouldn't have come to meet you."

Dunhuang knew Bao Ding didn't play mind games with his friends, and he let it go. He was out, that was the main thing. Bao Ding ordered one of everything he'd been missing, and they ate and drank and talked. He said the Hubei bastard would have a hard time of it, they were sure to extend his sentence, and it served him right for starting fights when he was already in jail. Bao Ding was lucky he stepped into the fight when he did, otherwise who knew where he might have been transferred to. He told a few fragmentary stories of funny things that had happened in jail, some of which Dunhuang had experienced himself, some of which he'd only seen on television, and some were even better than on TV. One guy who was a little wrong in the head kept yammering on about how he was going to commit suicide. He had his heart set on hanging himself but had no rope, and early every morning he would go around to the other prisoners' bunks and collect threads and lint, meaning to accumulate enough to braid himself a noose. Another guy collected all the dead insects he could, even lice. He squashed them flat and kept them, saying he'd eventually use them to piece together a map of the world.

By the time they'd put down fifteen bottles of beer Bao Ding was a little drunk. When they were paying the bill he suddenly asked, "Where's Qibao?"

"She might be making a delivery," said Dunhuang. "I'll tell her to come over." He called Qibao's number but her phone was off. "Why don't you go back and have a nap first?"

"Yeah," said Bao Ding. "This beer has gone to my head."

17

Bao Ding slept all afternoon in Dunhuang's room and woke at dusk. Dunhuang wasn't there. Under the bed was a pair of delicate women's slippers. He picked them up and smelled them for a while before putting them down and knocking them back under the bed with his heel. Before he finished a cigarette, Dunhuang was back. He was carrying an assortment of bags full of clothes he'd bought for Bao Ding, everything he'd need from head to toe, including a pair of leather sandals. "You're dressing me up for my wedding," said Bao Ding.

Dunhuang said, "You said a man's got to look good."

"Kid, I was talking about you," Bao Ding said.

The landlady wasn't home, so Dunhuang told Bao Ding to wash at the spigot in the yard while he kept watch at the main gate. It was dark by the time Bao Ding finished washing and dressing—he hardly recognized himself. "Damn," he said. "It's good to be out."

They ate dinner out. Dunhuang stuffed five hundred kuai in Bao Ding's pocket.

"What the hell is this?" Bao Ding asked.

"I'm going to deliver some DVDs in a bit," Dunhuang said. "If you go out, you ought to have something in your pocket."

"Fuck, kid, are you trying to corrupt me?"

Dunhuang chuckled. "I never said a word."

After they parted, Dunhuang called Qibao again, but her phone was still off. *That damned girl…*

Bao Ding wandered out, hands in his pockets, with no particular destination. Haidian district hadn't changed much. A string of cars were parked outside the sports arena; the wealthy were inside exercising, the young were singing karaoke. Same as always. Bao Ding's sudden freedom left him feeling empty, and he decided he needed something to do. He got on the number 332 bus. He rode all the way to Xizhimen, the last stop, then left the station and continued wandering. The streets were packed with people—what an enormous jail you'd need if you wanted to lock them all up. He followed the footsteps of others: turning around, going straight ahead, crossing the street, straight again, turning, crossing the street, and then he was standing in front of a small nightclub. Bao Ding looked at the flickering, shimmering neon and laughed. He shuffled his feet—*son of a bitch, they're all trying to corrupt me*. So that empty feeling had just been telling him to come here. Before jail he visited once or twice a month, it was a safe place.

The duty manager was a woman, a crumbling beauty. To his surprise she remembered him. She shook his hand and said, "It's been a while, have you been striking it rich?"

Bao Ding grinned, "I had some business to attend to, just got back."

"What'll it be? A little relaxation?"

Bao Ding laughed, and said he could use a rest. The manager said he'd be wanting a bed then, and signaled to another employee. Bao Ding followed the employee to another floor, where she pushed open the door of a room where a dozen girls in low-cut dresses were drinking and laughing. Bao

Ding pointed to the one with the lowest-cut dress and said, "That one."

"You don't want to take a closer look?"

"That one," Bao Ding repeated, then turned and continued on.

Seated on a sofa, he had a cigarette and fingered the money in his pocket. This place was aimed at working men, so he ought to have enough. The girl stuck her head through the door and asked innocently, "Did you ask for me?"

Bao Ding waved her in, and the moment she sat down he stubbed out his cigarette and said, "Strip." The girl blinked at his abruptness, and Bao Ding knew he was being a little hasty. *What could you do?* he thought. *You try going for six months without.*

Two rounds later, Bao Ding re-lit the cigarette he'd stubbed out. When he finished it, he wanted to use the toilet. As he got out of bed he said to the girl, Don't go anywhere, we're not done. She looked as if she might cry.

When Bao Ding was finished he came out of the men's room and headed for the sink to wash his hands, but a girl got there before him. She spat several times into the sink, then started washing her hands, while a man outside urged her to hurry up. "I'm coming," said the girl. Something inside Bao Ding went *clunk*, and he looked in the mirror: it was Qibao. Bao Ding hurried out of the washroom. After Qibao washed her hands she went into the ladies' room, and Bao Ding waited outside. Qibao—it had to be her. She washed her hands again, dried them, and as she came out the man waiting for her put his arm around her shoulder. Bao Ding followed behind, watching the man's hand slide down from her shoulder to her ass, and then they went into a private room and closed the door.

Bao Ding's mood was instantly fouled. When he returned to the room he dropped his trousers. "Be a little gentler, okay?" the girl said. He stared at her until she retreated under the covers. The blanket moved a bit, and the G-string she'd just put on slid out onto the floor. But Bao Ding turned and pulled his trousers back on. Before he left he dropped a hundred-kuai bill onto the G-string.

It was nearly midnight when he returned to Weixiuyuan. Dunhuang was at home, watching a film. He stood up when Bao Ding came in the door, saying, "I thought you weren't coming back." Bao Ding planted a foot in his chest, sending him sprawling back onto the bed.

"Bad enough that you screwed her," Bao Ding shouted, pointing at Dunhuang, his eyes bloodshot. "But did you have to let other guys screw her too? You call yourself a man?"

"You mean…Qibao?" Dunhuang clambered back up from the bed.

Bao Ding gave him another boot, knocking him back down. "Don't you fucking play the fool, she's your woman!"

Dunhuang stood up again, his fist in Bao Ding's face. "What the hell are you talking about?! What's wrong with Qibao?"

"She's a fucking nightclub girl!" Bao Ding suddenly collapsed in the chair, exhausted.

"What are you talking about?"

Bao Ding told him. There was no mistake, unless she had a twin sister. Dunhuang called her phone, it was still off. He put on his shoes, meaning to go to Huayuancun. Bao Ding said, "Forget it, worry about it tomorrow." Dunhuang shoved his hand away: "This has got nothing to do with you!"

Dunhuang took a taxi to Huayuancun. He pressed the intercom buzzer for ages, but no one answered. Bony Beauty wasn't at home either. Dunhuang waited outside, sleeping and waking in turns, until he was covered in dew.

At 5:10am, the sky already lightening, Qibao came back, a satchel over her shoulder. When she saw Dunhuang's dew-soaked hair and clothes, she subconsciously tugged at her dress.

Dunhuang's eyes were mean. "How long have you been doing it?"

"Doing what?" she asked.

Dunhuang's temper flared, and his palm hit her right cheek.

Qibao pulled back in shock, then gave him a slap in return. "What business is it of yours what I do?"

"We've been sleeping together this long, I should think it's my business! You're my goddamn woman!" Another ringing slap landed on her left cheek.

She returned the compliment, also on his left cheek. "Since when am I your woman! Did the Party Chairman sell me to you?"

Dunhuang delivered a third slap. "How fucking shameless can you get?"

Her response landed almost simultaneously. "Oh, so you feel shame, do you? When you're out fucking women? You, Bao Ding, Kuang Shan—which of you feels a scrap of fucking shame?"

"You sold it to Kuang Shan, too?"

"Yeah, I sold it. I sold it to anyone who was buying."

A year ago, Kuang Shan had gone to the same nightclub and requested her, and they'd gotten to know each other. After Dunhuang had treated him to dinner, he had called Qibao, but she wouldn't see him. "Are you afraid he'll find out?" asked Kuang Shan. "I can't speak for anyone else, but I can keep my mouth shut." They weren't strangers, after all, and he was paying. In the end she went to see him.

Early risers in the surrounding apartments watched from their windows as the young couple in the garden exchanged slaps. They were just getting into the show when the young man turned and walked away. Of course, they couldn't hear the last thing he said, "That's it. It's over."

18

Dunhuang kept selling DVDs. He didn't contact Qibao, and she didn't come to see him. Occasionally, he'd meet Xiaorong on the street or at the entrance to some supermarket. Her belly was impressive, given its size and how much time had passed, it could very well be twins. And if it were twins, which one would be called Kuang Xia? Xiaorong always had a small bag of DVDs with her, and as she spoke to her customers she'd glance from side to side. Kuang Shan smoked a little ways off, looking like an innocent bystander, a locked case at his feet. The rat bastard had been spooked, and was pushing Xiaorong and her belly out onto the front lines alone.

Bao Ding stayed in Dunhuang's room for two more days before renting a room of his own by Madian Bridge. He was back doing fake IDs, plenty of his old contacts were still around. When he was leaving, Dunhuang gave him 1,500 kuai, everything he'd saved, and Bao Ding didn't stand on ceremony. He told Dunhuang not to take it all to heart, in a place like Beijing anything could happen.

Life was simple once again. Dunhuang turned his full attention to his DVDs, selling them and watching them. He found a few new regular outlets, and sales were good—most importantly, it was safe. That was a piece of parting advice from Bao Ding—if you went to jail, you'd have to start all over again. After a day of making runs he'd return to his room, lie on his bed, and think of Qibao and Xiaorong, but only for a few moments before he put in a movie and started watching. Sometimes he'd look at the actresses and note their similarities to Qibao or Xiaorong, then berate himself for being pathetic. He was a man, wasn't he? Why couldn't he be a little more goddamn manly?

It seemed the rest of his life could easily pass this way.

One day at four in the morning he was awoken by his cellphone ringing. The movie he'd been watching was finished, and the screen was a pure blue. It was an unfamiliar number, and a woman's voice on the other end told him that Qibao had been caught. He asked who was calling. She wouldn't say, only adding that a dozen girls had been caught together. Dunhuang's first reaction was to ask, "How much will it cost?"

"Five thousand, more or less," she replied.

Things had finally blown up. After he hung up the phone Dunhuang realized the voice had been Bony Beauty. He should have known long ago they were in the same line of work—she must have dodged the sweep. Five thousand. An astronomical sum. Dunhuang called Bao Ding but his phone was off, so he got in a taxi and went looking for him. Bao Ding had been sleeping; as soon as he heard Dunhuang needed money he understood, "Qibao?" Dunhuang nodded. Bao Ding told him to go back and keep trying to think of solutions, he would talk to a couple of friends and see how much he could borrow. The longer they delayed the harder it would be. Dunhuang could think of nothing else but to visit Xiaorong and Kuang Shan in Furongli, they were his only friends. Xiaorong asked what had happened. Dunhuang wouldn't tell her, he only said he was in urgent need of a loan. Kuang Shan wanted to press the question but Dunhuang shot him an evil look, and he shut up.

"We've got that seventeen hundred," said Xiaorong. "You could take that for now."

"We were going to use that money to restock tomorrow," said Kuang Shan.

"It won't kill us to restock a few days later," she replied.

Dunhuang stared at Kuang Shan and pictured slapping him across the face. Kuang Shan reluctantly drew the money from a drawer. Dunhuang ignored him, and thanked Xiaorong.

By seven the next morning they'd collected six thousand three hundred kuai. They took a cab to the police station and were directed to the waiting area, where they sat until everyone's statements had been taken down. Bao Ding said to the police officer, "Girls from the countryside have it hard in jail, I hope to get her out as soon as possible."

The officer said, "None of us want to drag this crap out longer than necessary." They made their decision quickly, and there was no negotiating the price—five thousand. It was routine stuff, everyone knew that once the fine was paid the suspect would be released. It was a tedious process, that was all. Bao Ding helped Dunhuang though the formalities, but just before Qibao was released he said he had something to do, and left.

Dunhuang stood in the doorway, and watched Qibao, her hair in disarray, follow a policeman out. She kept her head down, and didn't raise it even when she was standing in front of him. Dunhuang tucked the hair hanging over her face behind one ear, then put an arm around her shoulder and said, "Let's go."

They were silent on the way back. When they arrived at Huayuancun, Bony Beauty opened the door. She said nothing when she saw them, and retreated to her own room. Qibao lay on the bed and lit a Zhongnanhai. Dunhuang snatched it from between her lips and hurled it out the window.

"Money, money…What the hell do you need so much money for?" Dunhuang couldn't stand it anymore. "Are you going to take it to your grave?"

"How can I make it without money?"

"Get out if you can't make it! Who says you've got to stick around here?"

Then the two of them fell silent. Strange noises emitted from Bony Beauty's room; this time it was the guy.

"That's it," said Dunhuang. "We're moving out of here."

The next day they moved to Mudanyuan, near north Taipingzhuang. It was a single-bedroom apartment, the rent was fair. Qibao gave up her place in Huanyuancun, and Dunhuang moved out of the room in Weixiuyuan. Qibao had just enough savings to pay back what Dunhuang had borrowed. Once they'd fixed the new place up they invited Bao Ding over for dinner. He looked the apartment over from top to bottom, then said, "Good; this is good. You'll make it bit by bit. A life of luxury is tough in this damned city, but you're not likely to starve, either." Then he said, "Hurry up and have a son. You'll have to do it sooner or later, so it might as well be sooner."

That was late June. Then it was July and August, the city's hottest months, and after that it began to cool. Both Dunhuang and Qibao had birthdays in August—Dunhuang was twenty-six, Qibao twenty-four. They picked a day halfway between their birthdays, bought a cake, and each ate half. Qibao made some dinner, they drank a few bottles of beer, and that was it for the celebration.

"If you add our ages together," said Dunhuang, "we're about halfway to dead."

"You can hardly handle a full round in bed anymore," teased Qibao. "Looks like you're more than halfway there."

"Doesn't matter, as long as we're happy," he said. "One day at a time."

August was a good month for them. Business was booming for both pirated DVDs and fake IDs. Dunhuang noticed that porn was selling particularly well, and he wondered to Qibao if the weather was turning all the boys and girls bad. They were in bed, and Qibao rolled over on top of him and said, "Maybe you should ask yourself that question."

Dunhuang said, "God, it's a veritable flood." Qibao's river was overflowing.

As he was selling DVDs one afternoon, Dunhuang heard someone calling his name. It was Kuang Shan, he had Xiaorong's DVD bag in his left hand, and his own case in his right. Xiaorong followed behind him, her belly enormous. They greeted each other, and Kuang Shan put Xiaorong's bag down a couple meters away, saying they'd set up shop next door.

"How's Qibao been?" asked Xiaorong.

"Same as always," answered Dunhuang. "Still doing IDs. How about you guys?"

"We got registered a few days ago. He got an old friend to help us do it."

"You're married? Congratulations! Why didn't you say something earlier?"

"We've been together for ages," said Kuang Shan, rubbing Xiaorong's belly. "We're too old to make a big fuss about it. Ha, I'm going to be a dad."

Xiaorong slapped his hand away and rubbed her own belly in satisfaction, her dimples showing tenderly. Kuang Xia wasn't even born yet, but Xiaorong already looked like a mother.

Dunhuang began going through his DVDs, and heard Kuang Shan say into his phone, "Yeah, I just got here... Okay. Okay."

Five minutes later, two kids with dyed red hair and saggy pants approached, and one of them snapped his fingers at Kuang Shan. Kuang Shan grinned at Dunhuang and said he'd be right back, he had a deal to do. He led the red-haired kids a dozen meters off, beneath a cedar tree. To one side was a subway stop construction site, all steel plates and disorderly heaps of sand, and a little passageway leading to the next street over. Dunhuang knew Kuang Shan had a big deal on his hands and didn't want to reveal his envy. As he was turning away, he saw Kuang Shan squat down and open his case, the kids drawing close around him. They looked through the contents, then closed the case and began speaking in low voices. The three huddled like that for a while. Xiaorong was anxious, and said to Dunhuang, "What's taking them so long? Can you go take a look for me?"

"Don't worry," said Dunhuang, "they're just haggling."

Before he'd finished speaking, two police officers appeared from the construction site's passageway. Dunhuang swiftly closed his bag, then ran over and helped Xiaorong gather her things. "We've got to go now," he said to her. Xiaorong, flustered, was still looking left and right.

The police had already reached Kuang Shan. "What's going on here!" they shouted. The red-haired kids leaped up and ran— the police caught only Kuang Shan and his case. Xiaorong panicked, one hand on her belly and the other trembling as she pointed at Kuang Shan. Her voice changed, "Kuang Shan! Dunhuang, quick, Kuang Shan!" He'd never seen a look like that on her face before. "Dunhuang, quickly! I'm begging you!"

By the time his bag hit the ground, he'd already reached

the police. He shouted "Hands off my DVDs!" at the top of his lungs, ripped the case out of the hands of one of the officers, and took off through the passageway, heading north. As he ran, he continued shouting, "My DVDs!" The police hadn't expected anything like that, they abandoned Kuang Shan and took off after Dunhuang. He sprinted, case in hand, while the police shouted at him to stop. He wasn't about to stop, though—he dodged around any corner he saw, and soon found that he'd made a full circle back to where they'd started. Xiaorong sat on the ground, a pool of red spreading between her legs, a few concerned bystanders gathered around and trying to help her up. Kuang Shan was nowhere in sight. He had meant to run past Xiaorong, but Dunhuang changed course suddenly, and the metal case banged against one knee, sending him sprawling—the case smashed to the ground and burst open, scattering garish DVDs everywhere. One of the bystanders shouted in surprise. Nearly every DVD cover featured a pair of smooth white legs, a pair of smooth white breasts.